W9-AEV-555

Mysteries of Thorn Manor

Also by Margaret Rogerson

An Enchantment of Ravens
Sorcery of Thorns
Vespertine

Mysteries of Thorn Manor

MARGARET ROGERSON

MARGARET K. McELDERRY BOOKS
New York   London   Toronto   Sydney   New Delhi

MARGARET K. McELDERRY BOOKS

An imprint of Simon & Schuster Children's Publishing Division

1230 Avenue of the Americas, New York, New York 10020

Text © 2023 by Margaret Rogerson

Jacket illustration © 2023 by Charlie Bowater

Jacket design by Sonia Chaghatzbanian © 2023 by Simon & Schuster, Inc.

MARGARET K. McELDERRY BOOKS is a trademark of Simon & Schuster, Inc.

For information about special discounts for bulk purchases, please contact Simon & Schuster Special Sales at 1-866-506-1949 or business@simonandschuster.com.

The Simon & Schuster Speakers Bureau can bring authors to your live event. For more information or to book an event, contact the Simon & Schuster Speakers Bureau at 1-866-248-3049 or visit our website at www.simonspeakers.com.

Interior design by Irene Metaxatos

The text for this book was set in Sabon LT Std.

Manufactured in the United States of America

First Edition

2 4 6 8 10 9 7 5 3 1

Library of Congress Cataloging-in-Publication Data

Names: Rogerson, Margaret, author.

Title: The mysteries of Thorn Manor / Margaret Rogerson.

Description: First edition. | New York : Margaret K. McElderry Books, 2023. | Audience: Ages 14 up. | Audience: Grades 10–12. | Summary: Elisabeth, Nathaniel, and Silas must unravel the magical trap keeping them inside Thorn Manor in time for their Midwinter Ball.

Identifiers: LCCN 2022030707 (print) | LCCN 2022030708 (ebook) | ISBN 9781665935616 (hardcover) | ISBN 9781665935623 (ebook)

Subjects: CYAC: Magic—Fiction. | Blessing and cursing—Fiction. | Interpersonal relations—Fiction. | Fantasy. | LCGFT: Fantasy fiction. | Novels.

Classification: LCC PZ7.1.R6635 My 2023 (print) | LCC PZ7.1.R6635 (ebook) | DDC [Fic]—dc23

LC record available at https://lccn.loc.gov/2022030707

LC ebook record available at https://lccn.loc.gov/2022030708

To those who believe in
fairy-tale endings

ONE

"I DIDN'T DO THIS!" Nathaniel insisted, leaning out the manor's front door, gazing helplessly at the vines thrashing up along the thorn hedge, the animated topiaries prowling through the garden, and the threatening magical gale that howled around Thorn Manor, carrying past leaves and branches and loose cobblestones in a whirling cyclone. "I swear upon Baltasar's unholy grave, I didn't do a thing."

Elisabeth gave him a skeptical look. "Most of the time when you say that, it turns out that actually—"

"Yes, yes, I know."

"Like when it started raining teacups on Laurel Avenue—"

"I thought we agreed not to talk about that."

"And the time a lightning strike blew off one of the Magisterium's towers—"

"Point taken. But I didn't have another nightmare last night, did I? You certainly would have noticed."

She felt herself turn pink. "No. You didn't."

He grinned at her, looking unfairly handsome in just his nightshirt, with his sleeves billowing and his dark hair whipped in every direction by the wind. "Anyway, all of this must have something to do with the manor's wards. Look at the street past the gates, it's completely normal."

She squinted through the streaks of swirling debris, and saw that he was right. The rest of Hemlock Park appeared to be enjoying a sunny, peaceful February morning. That failed to ease her mind. Especially because, standing just past the cyclone, a crowd had gathered; and at the very front stood a group of—

"Reporters," Nathaniel said darkly.

"Elisabeth Scrivener!" they called out in excitement, noticing that the front door had opened. "Magister Thorn! Would you care to comment on the situation? Have you lost control of your magic? Is it true that your demon is back?"

Nathaniel only frowned. Then another reporter shouted, "Is this likely to impact your preparations for the Midwinter Ball next w—"

Elisabeth didn't hear the rest, because Nathaniel had hastily drawn her inside and slammed the door behind them.

"You know, I find that I don't mind it a great deal after all," he said later that day, cheerfully watching a shrub sail past the foyer's window. "In fact, I believe the view is growing on me."

"You can't leave it this way forever," Elisabeth pointed out. "It's trapping us inside, too. We'll starve. Also, that looks like it came off the roof."

Nathaniel used his cane to slide the curtain open a little wider, watching with interest as a giant chunk of masonry went spinning by. The crowd of spectators screamed and ducked. If anything, Nathaniel only looked more pleased.

"Oh, I'm sure we have enough provisions to last us a few weeks. And if the roof starts leaking, I can simply use magic . . . Scrivener?" he asked in alarm. "Where are you going?"

She didn't answer, because she had drawn Demon-slayer and charged out the door.

A moment later she charged back inside, chased by an army of vines swarming at her heels, their dagger-length thorns clattering angrily across the foyer's tiles. She was wild-eyed, with leaves tangled in her hair.

"Their heads grow back!" she shouted, hacking at the vines.

"Of course they do!" Nathaniel yelled. "They're magical topiaries! I could have told you that, if you hadn't charged outside to fight them in your pajamas!" He summoned a gout of emerald fire that burnt several vines to ashes, filling the room with the potent stink of aetherial combustion. But it didn't seem to help. As soon as the ashes pattered to the floor, another wave of vines swarmed inside to fill the gap.

They stretched from the hedge all the way indoors, their numbers inexhaustible. The more Elisabeth hacked at them, and the more Nathaniel scorched them with fireballs, the more they multiplied like the heads of a hydra. The tide of battle finally turned when Mercy emerged from the hall, let out a full-throated battle cry, and whacked the vines with a broom. This seemed to work for a moment, if only due to the element of surprise: the hedge shrank back, appearing rather shocked. Before it could rally, Elisabeth forced her way to the door and shoved it shut with all her strength, slamming it on a single thorny tendril that had enterprisingly snaked back inside. When it refused to retreat, she lopped off the end with her sword.

They all stood watching in silent horror as the vine flopped around on the carpet, still alive. Eventually Mercy had the presence of mind to trap it beneath an overturned dustbin.

"Suppose we're stuck inside, then," she observed as the dustbin hopped and rattled furiously across the carpet.

"So it would appear," said Nathaniel cheerfully. "How terribly inconvenient. It'll take me weeks to sort this out."

Elisabeth paused, remembering what the reporter had started to say earlier, and then rounded on him. "What is the Midwinter Ball?"

He was busy dusting burnt-up vine ash off his sleeves. "Trust me, Scrivener, you're better off not knowing. Imagine being stuffed into a sorcerer's fusty old ballroom, where the chandeliers are enchanted to drip wax on anyone who criticizes the hors d'oeuvres, and getting tortured to death with small talk for hours."

"It is a social occasion, mistress," contributed a whispering voice from the hall.

"Exactly," Nathaniel said.

Sometimes, Elisabeth still felt a frisson of surprise when Silas appeared. Standing in the hallway's shadows, he looked like a ghost, and it was easy to imagine him as one—pale, insubstantial, his narrow silhouette poised to melt into the wainscoting at any moment. She had difficulty shaking the idea that he was a figment of her imagination, or even an illusion conjured by Nathaniel during one of his nightmares. But he was undeniably real. She had touched him. Earlier, he had served her breakfast.

She couldn't make out his face, but she got the impression he was trying his best not to look at the layer of ash coating the foyer's tiles—or, for that matter, notice the dustbin juddering its way determinedly toward the parlor. He continued softly, "It is a yearly tradition among sorcerers, meant to uphold the relations between houses. Every winter, a different magister is chosen to host the ball."

Elisabeth evaluated Nathaniel in suspicion. Over the past few weeks, she had caught him feeding formal-looking letters into the fire. "You're supposed to host it this year, aren't you?"

"I don't see why I should." He had gone back to dusting off his sleeves. "Until barely two months ago, I was no longer a sorcerer."

Her eyes narrowed. "Are you trying to get out of it by using the manor's wards?"

"No, but I wish I'd thought of that. Brilliant, isn't it?" Outside, someone screamed.

"Reporter," Mercy declared, peering through the curtains. "Still alive."

"More's the pity," Nathaniel said.

At some point Silas had stepped into the light, though Elisabeth hadn't seen him move. His marble-white features looked no less unearthly in the late-afternoon glow leaking through the leaded panes, which winked with the shapes of debris swooping past, casting flickers of shadow across the foyer's checkered tiles. "Perhaps we might retire to the dining room. I have prepared your supper, which is growing cold."

His soft voice held no indication of a threat. Never-theless, everyone scrambled to obey.

The dining room proved to be turned out in rare style even for Silas. Lit tapers reflected on the long table's polished walnut surface and glimmered from a profu-sion of silver utensils and tureens. Each place had been formally set with fine porcelain and jade chargers—not just their three places, but the table's full complement of eighteen. Mercy hesitated at the threshold before stiffly taking a seat, her face grimly set, as though preparing herself for battle.

Elisabeth's brow furrowed in concern, but then Silas returned with a platter in his hands, and her mind disintegrated at the smell. She had devoured three por-tions of flaky white fish, lost in the spice of the ginger sauce and the delicate crunch of snow peas, before she regained the capacity for rational thought. When she finally looked up, Nathaniel was prodding his meal with his fork.

She felt a twinge of sympathy. The prospect of pub-licly reemerging into magical society couldn't be easy for him. Not after his injury, and the reporters, and the questions circulating about his sorcery. But her good-will promptly vanished when the conversation turned to fixing the wards, and he pretended to go to sleep.

"If no one gave them orders, why would they have woken up?" Mercy asked after an uncertain glance at Nathaniel, who was sprawled across his chair, snoring extravagantly. "Is the manor trying to tell us that we'll be in danger if we leave the house? It isn't something like Ashcroft again, is it?" By now she had been filled in on nearly every detail of last autumn's events.

Silas glanced at her beneath his lashes. Elisabeth tensed. She couldn't explain it, but for some reason a jolt of alarm shot through her every time he acknowledged Mercy's presence, even though he'd been nothing but polite to her ever since he'd returned and found her working as a servant in the manor.

To her obscure relief, he only said, "Not necessarily, miss. Ancient spells such as the ones laid down in this manor's foundations often grow temperamental with age. I believe it is more likely that something has occurred to trigger a minor modification to the wards. Sorcerers have added their own clauses over time, some of which are quite specific. Can any of you think of anything out of the ordinary you have done in the past twenty-four hours?"

He asked this in a very mild tone of voice, but at once everyone turned to look at Nathaniel, who proved that he was awake by opening his eyes and sputtering in protest.

"Well, I can't," Mercy said stoutly.

"I was in the study all day yesterday, working," Elisabeth put in.

"I was barely home!" Nathaniel exclaimed. "I was at the Magisterium consulting on Ashcroft's artifacts. I didn't get back until well after dark, and then—"

The two of them exchanged a look, remembering.

"What is it?" Mercy asked.

"Nothing," Elisabeth said quickly. And really, it couldn't be important. She had slept in Nathaniel's room plenty of times before; she had done it nearly every night during his recovery, so she could be there to help him if he needed to get up to use the water closet or started having a nightmare. The wards hadn't objected *then*. Granted, she had been sleeping on the floor, and most of the time they hadn't been touching each other . . .

But it wasn't as though they'd done anything last night. Just a little kissing. A few minutes of kissing, and then they'd gone to sleep.

"Indeed," said Silas ambiguously. "In that case, master, I recommend that we retire for the evening, and discuss this more tomorrow."

Silas insisted on drawing Elisabeth a bath, which she had to admit wasn't unwarranted as she watched the water in the copper tub turn brown, swirling with bits of leaves. At least he hadn't made her wash her hair; he had relented to her protestations with a sigh, and placed an ivory comb on the nightstand instead.

When she had finally succeeded in conquering her unruly tangles, she soaked for a while with her eyes closed, listening to the soft sounds as he moved around the room, opening and closing drawers. Then she forced herself to sit up, her arms clamped over her chest as still-steaming water sluiced from her skin. Silas had laid a towel over the folding screen and placed a clean set of nightclothes across the foot of the bed. Craning her neck, she could see him just beyond the screen's edge: he stood turned away, casting a critical gaze over her ruined clothes, which hung limply from his hands.

She rarely got the chance to look at him without him noticing. Silently, she studied him in the lilac room's gauzy light. Upon cursory inspection, he looked exactly the same as he had before that fateful night in the Royal Library, his alabaster beauty untouched. But Nathaniel was convinced that he had been injured by the Archon. He couldn't explain how he knew, only that he could sense Silas's unwellness like a shadow at the corner of his mind.

Silas had never revealed how he had survived the confrontation, or what had happened to him afterward in the Otherworld. If Elisabeth watched him steadily enough without interruption, she began to grow aware of something different about him, though she couldn't explain exactly what: only that he seemed to fade, to become thinner and more insubstantial. At times she imagined she glimpsed pain lurking deep in his yellow eyes, as difficult to interpret as the impassive gaze of a wounded feline.

Whatever ailed him, she was glad Mercy worked here now, so he didn't have to do everything on his own. As soon as she had the thought, she regretted thinking it. Silas was as adept at reading her as ever. His eyes flicked to hers, and his lips thinned.

"Isn't it better to have help?" she blurted out. "It's just—it's a big house. You don't have to do everything alone." *You don't have to do it at all,* she didn't add, for the matter had already been raised, and Silas had insisted on resuming his role as a servant with a strange brittle intensity that had put an end to the discussion immediately.

"As you say, mistress," he said. He helped her step out of the bath, wrapping the towel around her shoulders with his eyes averted. Then he gave a slight bow, and left.

Elisabeth bit her lip. She dried herself off and tugged on her nightgown, followed by the matching silk dressing gown. When she was done, she caught her own reflection in the mirror, rippling across the glass: the cream-colored silk trimmed with a pattern of spring vines, her unbound hair shining in waves nearly to her waist. She touched the silver strands glittering among the brown, representing the single day of life that Silas had taken from her—a match for Nathaniel's own token payment. Out of habit, she lifted Demonslayer from her nightstand. Then, before she paused to think, she made her way down the hallway to Nathaniel's bedroom.

She had said something to offend Silas, but she didn't know what, or at least why. As she padded down the hall, she reflected that she wondered many things about him that might never have answers. She wondered if, when he walked into the Archon's circle to sacrifice himself, he had thought Nathaniel might die anyway. Nathaniel almost had. She wondered how he had felt when he came back to find Nathaniel alive, and whether, during all those weeks he'd waited for a summoning that never came, he took it as proof that the worst had come to pass. Most of all, she wondered if he noticed the pall of grief that had filled the manor like cobwebs in his absence; if he knew how much he had been missed. She hoped that he did. But there were some things she couldn't talk to Silas about. She saw the look in his yellow eyes, and knew it would be like touching him with iron.

When she appeared in Nathaniel's doorway, he was sitting on the edge of the bed, gazing toward the darkened window in thought. She lingered outside, overwhelmed by a sudden shyness. Even though she had been present for every stage of his recovery, she often found herself feeling newly tentative around him in private. Everything he had endured at Ashcroft's hands seemed to have made him older, more mysterious, more powerful—a man and not a boy, as though over the past months he had crossed some invisible threshold to adulthood. This was easy enough to overlook when he was being ridiculous—which, granted, accounted for most hours of the day—but when they were alone together, the humor with which he armored himself temporarily set aside, she found it burningly impossible to ignore.

Standing there, she must have made a sound. He looked up and paused, taking her in. He didn't appear at all surprised to find her holding a sword at the entrance to his bedroom. His eyes were very dark, his hair slightly damp. Her stomach performed a sort of effervescent tumble, like an ice cube dropped into a fizzing glass of champagne.

"You might as well sleep here again," he said, still watching her intently. "If a topiary comes crashing through the window, we may need to fight it off together."

Elisabeth eyed the bed. It was a great monstrosity

with its four carved posters and embroidered hangings and piled-up pillows, more than large enough for two. "But you don't think we caused this by sleeping together? Sleeping in the same bed, I mean, and kissing."

"It isn't as though we've never kissed in this room before," Nathaniel pointed out, his eyebrows rising. Her cheeks flamed. With some effort, she managed not to glance at the window seat. "And even if we did offend the house with our shocking indiscretions," he went on, "the damage is already done. I hardly imagine we can make it any worse."

She wasn't so sure about that, but she moved toward the other side of the bed anyway, hung up her dressing gown, and slipped beneath the covers. Demonslayer went beside the nightstand, within easy reach. "No kissing," she said. "Just in case."

He rolled over to face her. "Yes, my terror," he said obediently, with a wicked sparkle in his eyes.

She took one of the pillows and placed it firmly between them, which made Nathaniel laugh. He snapped his fingers, and the hangings slid free from their ties to close with a quiet swish around the bed, shutting them out from the world.

TWO

ELISABETH AWOKE LATER in the dark, with nothing on her mind whatsoever except for the warmth of Nathaniel's body very close, almost touching; she felt the loose fabric of her nightgown brushing against him slightly as she breathed in and out, and suddenly she grew aware of every place the silky fabric touched her skin. She could smell the soap he used, mixed with his own warm scent. His hair was tickling her nose. When she moved her head a fraction, there was his face, barely an inch from her own.

He appeared completely relaxed except for a deep groove between his eyebrows. It made him look serious but a little lost, as though his dreams had left him wandering in unfamiliar places. She leaned forward and kissed the spot gently. When she pulled back, he was awake, watching her.

"Scrivener," he said gravely. "It appears you missed."

And then they were kissing, urgent and fumbling. Her nose smashed clumsily against his, and her foot got tangled in the sheets, and her elbows were banging everything—but it didn't matter. He obviously didn't care. At one point they both nearly tumbled off the bed, which was when a single lucid thought pierced her mind's fog like a sunbeam: the pillow. Wasn't there supposed to be a pillow?

As soon as she remembered, the sound of the wind moaning around the manor rose to a dangerous howl. There came a series of fateful bangs and rattles from above, like something had gone careening across the roof.

They both froze, looking at each other. Elisabeth's lips tingled, and Nathaniel's breath feathered her face in the dark. Neither of them spoke, waiting to see if the noise would stop.

It didn't.

"I think we should check the roof," she whispered finally.

He flopped back on the bed, then groaned and reached for his cane. "You might want to bring Demonslayer."

She poked her nose outside the hangings and instantly regretted it. Nathaniel's bedroom was frigid. "Where are we going?" she asked as she pulled on her dressing gown, and then wrapped one of the bed's blankets around herself for good measure.

Ominously, he replied, "The attic."

Elisabeth had never seen the attic. Bending, she retrieved Demonslayer. Then she curiously followed Nathaniel down the hall, which proved even colder than his room. The ancient house groaned and shuddered around them like a ship tossed by a storm. When she paused to part the curtains and peer outside, great sheets of snow were whipping past, obscuring the view.

The entrance to the attic turned out to be a servants' door at the end of the hall. Beyond it lay an old, narrow stair, inside which the temperature dropped even further: their breath floated as ghostly clouds in the gloom. Nathaniel passed her a taper, lighting it with a muttered incantation. The wick flared green, casting an eerie light over the crooked steps, their treads coated in a thick layer of dust.

The stairs creaked in complaint at their ascent. She followed closely behind Nathaniel as he limped upward, ready to catch him if his leg gave out; it was only in the past month that he had begun managing stairs unassisted.

The rattle grew louder the nearer they drew to the attic. Only a loose shingle, she told herself, even though it sounded like a demon crouched on the roof, trying to scrabble its way inside. Her heart pounded as Nathaniel opened a second door at the top of the stairs, revealing a dark, yawning space. And then she gazed around in wonder.

The ruffling, draft-blown flame of the taper illuminated a museum-like jumble of objects receding into darkness: shrouded furniture, giant tarnished mirrors, a child's rocking horse, traveling chests, old-fashioned coats and dresses hanging on brass clothing racks, a box of creepy-looking dolls, a suit of medieval armor on a stand, and bizarrely, an entire carriage. After a moment she recognized the carriage as the one she had ridden in with Nathaniel, and realized she had never asked what he did with it when he wasn't using it. She supposed he must vanish it up here by magic. Cobwebs hung above like tattered streamers, drifting in the wind that whistled through the cracks. It was very cold, and everything smelled strongly of dust.

"Be careful," Nathaniel advised when she started for the suit of armor. "You can look around, but don't touch anything. I was never allowed to play up here as a child—some of the objects are cursed."

Elisabeth gripped Demonslayer's hilt as she inched past the box of dolls. "We should come up again during the daytime." When Nathaniel raised his eyebrows at her, she explained, "There might be a weapon to go along with the armor."

"That's just what we need, for you to get hold of a broadsword cursed by one of my evil ancestors. Scrivener, I know this goes against your red-blooded warrior nature, but if you see anything pointy, please make an effort to resist."

She barely heard him. She was wondering if the armor would fit her. It looked about the right size. She leaned close enough that her breath misted the metal, which was carved all over with an intricate pattern of thorns.

A faint, rusty-sounding squeak pierced the attic's

quiet as the helmet's visor turned to look at her, shedding trickles of dust. She leaped back, her hair standing on end. She had to swallow several times before she could speak, staring hard at the armor, which now stood perfectly still again, as though it had never moved at all. "Nathaniel—"

"It's cursed," he said, without even turning to look. He was scribbling something on one of the beams with a piece of chalk he'd fetched from his dressing gown.

Elisabeth glanced at the rocking horse.

"Also cursed," Nathaniel said, still without turning around.

"Why would someone curse a rocking horse?"

"I see you never met Great-Grandfather Wolfram. As luck would have it, neither did I." He then lapsed into a state of concentration that Elisabeth knew not to interrupt. An emerald glow spread from his hand, onto the beam and up toward the roof. Thankfully, whatever he was doing seemed to be working. The rattling began to subside.

Elisabeth stood stiffly in the exact middle of the path between the objects. She scowled at the rocking horse and then gave the dolls a challenging glare. They didn't move. Just as she began to relax, her eyes landed on something odd in one corner, a pale smear in the shadows, which bore a familiar assemblage of shapes: the dark hollows of eyes, a slash of a mouth. She lifted her taper. A wattled visage swam vaguely into view, suspended in the darkness behind the carriage. Without hesitation, she raised Demonslayer.

"Nathaniel," she whispered. "Nathaniel. There's a goblin in your attic."

"What? Oh." He laughed. "No, that's just Aunt Clothilde."

"She's alive?"

For some reason, that made Nathaniel laugh even harder. He must have cast a spell, because the candle blazed higher, its emerald flame bright enough to illuminate the picture frame surrounding the ghastly face, which Elisabeth now saw was only a portrait.

"I should have warned you. Silas put it there. The two of them have quite the history, I suspect." She heard the tap of his cane and then felt his warmth at her back. "You know, you might be onto something—I wonder if she actually *was* part goblin. I should ask Silas if . . . if that's . . ."

He trailed off. During his recovery he had often said things like *I should ask Silas about that* or *Whatever will Silas think?* only to remember that Silas was gone, and was never coming back. But this time, the light only dimmed in his eyes for a moment, and he cleared his throat when he noticed Elisabeth watching him. She wasn't sure what kind of expression she had on her face, but she felt like her heart had swelled up like a wet sponge, so it was probably an embarrassing one.

"As I was saying," he continued, "I'm certain Silas would simply love to tell us about the history of carnal knowledge between humans and—mff."

Elisabeth had firmly placed a hand over his mouth.

They went trooping back downstairs. As they passed the grandfather clock in the hall, they discovered it was already early morning. It only looked like the middle of the night because the storm was blocking out the sky.

They found Mercy downstairs in the parlor, awkwardly holding a pan of swept-out ashes from the fireplace as though she had nowhere to dump them— and perhaps she didn't, if she couldn't get outside.

"It wasn't me!" Nathaniel exclaimed as she turned a baleful eye in his direction. "Honestly, why does everyone always think it was me," he went on, exasperated, missing the look Elisabeth and Mercy traded behind his back as he limped past them toward the hall. "Not *just* me, anyway," he added under his breath.

The tantalizing aroma of baking scones lured everyone to the kitchen. Though Silas must have heard them coming, he didn't turn around when they crowded inside. He had opened the door that led out to the garden and was staring at the solid wall of snow packed against the house with an expression of deep reproach. He shut the door firmly and then did something Elisabeth had never seen before: he gave a little shudder, just like a cat confronted with the cold. Nathaniel caught her eye, grinning.

"Did you discover anything enlightening last night, master?" Silas inquired, turning his head slightly in their direction.

Elisabeth blushed. Nathaniel threw up his hands. "Fine! I'll help fix the wards. I do have some standards, contrary to popular opinion. I'm not about to sit back and watch my house turn into a prude."

"You had best fortify your standards with breakfast, in that case. Good morning, mistress. Mercy."

A short intake of breath answered. Mercy was standing behind them, her features frozen with wariness. Elisabeth didn't have long to puzzle over the other girl's expression. When she looked back, Silas's gaze had fallen to the dusty footprints deposited by her and Nathaniel's slippers on the kitchen's floorboards.

A tussle ensued. "I'll get that!" Elisabeth exclaimed, lunging for a rag, at the same time Mercy shouted, "Let me!" They fought over the rag until Elisabeth banged her head on the table. When she finished blinking away stars, the rag had vanished and Silas was using it to wipe the floor.

"I see I must remind you once more that I am not an invalid," he remarked, sending them a remonstrative look beneath his eyelashes.

Everyone exchanged glances. They had collectively agreed that they should all be doing more around the house so Silas could get more rest. But he'd caught on instantly; not only could he essentially read their minds, the discovery of Nathaniel having folded his own clothes was apparently both unprecedented and extremely suspicious.

An awkward silence fell. Nathaniel alleviated it by

saying, "Look, Elisabeth—I think your head dented the table." Everyone leaned closer to see. And sure enough, it had.

A few minutes later, after an embarrassing explanation to Mercy about the wards, breakfast was served. Elisabeth found that she didn't mind the storm howling outside, sitting in the warm, cozy kitchen with a fire crackling in the hearth and the smell of scones filling the air. Silas served them with apricot jam and peppermint tea, and even folded up the napkins in the shape of flowers, to which Nathaniel said, "Stop trying to intimidate Mercy, for heaven's sake, Silas." Silas bowed in assent; he didn't even try to deny it.

Mercy's face turned red. Dismayed, Elisabeth remembered last night's dinner and wondered if Silas had been doing the same thing then, too. She could still picture Mercy's expression as she took a seat: not surprise, but rather the grim endurance of someone who had been weathering a hardship for some time. Had this been going on for an entire month and a half, right beneath her nose? She looked at Silas in shock. Unaffected, he lifted the kettle from the fire using a carefully folded napkin—it wasn't the heat that posed a threat to him, she knew, but rather the fact that it was made of iron.

"Silas," she said impulsively, "is there any way you can help us with the wards? Even just a little."

He paused, then said, "Certainly, mistress," bowed again, and left the kitchen. Nathaniel muttered something that sounded like "favoritism."

Elisabeth waited until Silas had gone to place a tentative hand on Mercy's arm. "You know he's nothing like Mr. Hob." Until Silas, the only demon Mercy had encountered was the goblin masquerading as Ashcroft's butler.

"I know, miss," she said quietly.

"He's a completely different type of demon. A good one."

Mercy fiddled with her spoon, not quite meeting Elisabeth's eyes. "I know. He helped you save the world and whatnot, and he's been decent to me, and all. But miss—"

"Elisabeth," Elisabeth said.

Mercy snuck a sidelong look at Nathaniel. Then she lowered her voice even further. "It's just, Master Thorn—he ordered Silas not to kill me."

Beside them, Nathaniel coughed loudly into his tea. "You weren't supposed to hear that," he rasped once he had caught his breath.

"Neither were you just now," Mercy shot back. "Anyway," she went on resolutely, "I was standing outside in the hall when you said it."

A crumb dropped from the bite of scone in Elisabeth's hand, forgotten on its way to her mouth. "What? When did this happen?" she demanded, glancing back and forth between them.

Nathaniel grimaced. "I wasn't being serious, Mercy, for the most part."

"For the most part," Mercy repeated, staring.

"Silas would never kill you," Elisabeth insisted, barely able to believe she was saying those words out loud. He wouldn't. Would he? Then again . . .

The thirty years she and Nathaniel had sworn to him last time had been lost when he'd sacrificed himself. To replace it, he had only taken two days of their lives. At the time, she had assumed his nature had changed along with his name, and he no longer craved human life. But what if that wasn't true? What if he was hungry?

A cool breeze teased her hair. "There is no such thing

as a good demon, mistress," Silas interjected softly, bending past her to place something on the table. "Merely those who have manners, and those who do not."

None of them had heard him return. Mercy started visibly; even Elisabeth, who was no longer afraid of him, found herself gripped by a prey animal's instinctive reaction to a predator: goose bumps prickled along her arms as his silvery hair brushed past, and as his pale, clawed fingers slid away from the cloth-wrapped bundle he'd set between the teacups.

Nathaniel, who wouldn't so much as flinch if Silas ambushed him in a haunted crypt, was obviously grateful to change the subject. "If that's another gingerbread loaf, give it to Elisabeth. I'm trying to maintain my dainty figure."

Elisabeth sat up and eyed the rectangular bundle with interest, remembering the gingerbread Silas had baked for them during the holidays. But as soon as she hopefully sniffed the air, she knew what was really inside, and felt both a thrill of excitement and a cold touch of foreboding. "It doesn't smell friendly."

"I take it we aren't still discussing gingerbread," Nathaniel said. "Or are we? Is it one of those loaves shaped like a person, that's enchanted to run around screaming in terror until you hack it up with a knife? Sorcerer tradition," he explained to Mercy and Elisabeth, who were looking at him in horror.

"No," Elisabeth said. "It's a grimoire."

THREE

"STAY BACK," SHE warned. "It isn't friendly."

Friendly grimoires had a sort of sweet, custardy old-book smell; this one smelled sour, like spoiled milk. Everyone held their breath as she drew the bundle closer, parting the cloth. It was a small, slim grimoire, about the size of a journal. Gilt lettering stood out on its cracked leather spine: Volume XI. That was all she had a chance to see before it exploded into a frenzy of flapping pages. She snatched it and wrestled it back down to the table, pinning it beneath her weight, before it could go careening around the room.

"This is a Class Four," she said in surprise. "It should be in a library." After weeks spent rehabilitating the books in Nathaniel's study, she was intimately familiar with each of Thorn Manor's grimoires. At least, so she had thought. She certainly hadn't seen this one before. "Silas, where did you find it?"

"It has been living for some time as a feral on the fifth floor, mistress. The servants' floor," he explained, at her look of confusion. "I believe it escaped from the muniment room."

Elisabeth hadn't even known the manor had a fifth floor, much less something called a muniment room. Evidently, she wasn't alone. Nathaniel's eyebrows had risen. "The what?"

"The muniment room, master. It was closed in 1792 after your grandfather deemed it out of fashion, which may pose certain challenges, but you will find that it contains a record of every change made to the wards since the manor's construction in the sixteenth century." He inclined his head toward the grimoire.

Being pinned for a while seemed to have settled it down. Carefully, Elisabeth lifted its cover, wincing at the crackle of ancient parchment—but nothing seemed damaged, and there weren't any more worrisome sounds as she pried up more of the pages, peering inside. At first it only seemed to contain lists of mundane changes made to the manor and its grounds, renovations and the like, written and dated in a cramped, unpleasant-looking hand. But then she came to a magical diagram: a complex inscription of interlocking runes and geometric shapes, which floated up an inch or so off the page as she opened the grimoire the rest of the way, glowing a pale luminous blue. And it *moved*, the shapes revolving in midair like the gears on the inside of a clock, surrounded by scrolling circles of Enochian text. Elisabeth gasped. Even Mercy, who was rarely enchanted by magic, leaned forward for a look.

"It's a model of a household ward," Nathaniel said. Blue light illuminated the angular planes of his face and glittered in his gray eyes as he bent close, scanning the text. "That's exactly what they look like down in the foundations. I think this one is the ward for keeping trespassers out of the garden. My father had it deactivated during a renovation; I seem to recall there was an unfortunate incident with Lady Throckmorton's lapdog."

"Why can't we just go look at the wards themselves?" Elisabeth asked, surprised she hadn't thought of that before—but then again, until now, she had envisioned the wards as intangible layers of spells draped invisibly over the manor, not physical arrays like the summoning circle on the second floor.

"It's dangerous to expose them. They were created by old sorcery, the kind that's been illegal since the Reforms. And they're sealed in under hundreds of tons of stone. I only saw one once because my father had to rebuild the floor after the cellar flooded. It was a whole production—the Magisterium sent dozens of officials to supervise. So if we do end up having to look at them, it will only be as a last resort." He steepled his hands and pressed his mouth against them, staring hard at the grimoire. "The muniment room—where can we find it?"

"The door is located beside the bust of Erasmus Thorn, near the south parlor." A fleeting smile touched Silas's face. "I wish you both the best of luck."

"What did he mean when he said it had been closed?" Elisabeth asked, curiously eyeing the empty wood paneling beside Erasmus's bust. There wasn't a door to be seen.

Nathaniel was pacing back and forth in front of the

blank wall in a waistcoat and shirtsleeves, his cane rapping on the floor. He had tried muttering a few spells, but none of them seemed to have worked; all he had to show for his trouble was a faint stench of sorcery hanging in the air.

"Have you ever noticed that the manor seems larger on the inside than it does on the outside? Many of the rooms were created by sorcery, and when the current master of the house doesn't have a use for them any longer, he—or she, in some cases—orders them closed." He knelt with a quiet hiss of pain to examine the baseboards. "In ordinary houses, that would involve covering the furniture and locking the doors, but in sorcerous houses, we vanish the rooms outright. Apparently there's even a ballroom hidden away somewhere, but I've never been able to find it."

Elisabeth had no idea what Nathaniel was doing. Perhaps he was looking for a hidden latch of some kind. "Where do they go when no one's using them?"

"I think they get folded up inside the walls." Nathaniel got down all the way to the floor, pressed his cheek against the parquet, and peered intently into a crack. "Have you ever seen those paper dollhouses, the ones that open up from inside a book? It's just like that, or at least that's how my mother explained it to me."

Elisabeth knew right away what he was talking about. She had seen a dollhouse like that once—but it had been a grimoire, not an ordinary book. A sorcerer had made it for his sickly daughter, who died before it was completed. It had been transferred to Summershall for refurbishment, and the Director had shown it to Elisabeth when she was very small, only five or six, so the memory had a dreamlike quality: the way the huge gilt tome opened with a tiny key that the sorcerer had fashioned for his daughter to wear around her neck, just like a librarian, and then how the pages had fanned open on their own, revealing room after room, the folded-up pieces of furniture unfurling from the paper walls. There had been windows with shutters that opened and closed, with real light filtering through the curtains, the color of which changed according to the time of day. The wallpaper and the upholstery on the furniture had been carefully painted. And there had even been sounds: the tinkling of a harpsichord in the music room, the crackling of a fire in the study, the singing of a caged songbird in the conservatory.

The very last room had been a miniature of a little girl's bedroom. But in that room, there had been no sound at all, only silence.

"We should go looking for them," she said, struck by the same tingling flush of wonder that she had felt looking at that grimoire, the same sharp tug upon her heart. "I wonder if they're like the passageway in the Royal Library—the one that took us to the archives. Nathaniel," she added, frowning, "is your house actually alive, like the Royal Library?"

She missed his reply, because as soon as she asked that question, she saw the door.

It resolved from the paneling at the corner of her eye. Its outline shimmered faintly, like a mirage, and when she whipped around to look at it directly, it vanished. But as she stared hard at the wall, glaring it into submission, it slowly melted back into existence in a sort of abashed, caught-out way. Dust coated its doorknob and molding, as though it hadn't been disturbed in decades. And on the front there was a tarnished brass plate stamped with the words "Muniment Room."

"Thank you," Elisabeth said formally to the door. She supposed one ought to be polite to potentially sentient magical houses, as well as books.

"There's no need to thank me, Scrivener," Nathaniel said from the floor. He was still peering into cracks in the baseboard, creeping along on his hands and knees. "I'll get down on all fours for you whenever you like."

Without taking her eyes from the door, Elisabeth reached down, took him by the arm, and lifted him to his feet.

"Ah," he said, enlightened. "Of course, I should have guessed—your resistance to magic makes it difficult for the rooms to hide themselves from you. Though it does seem you had to bully it a little," he added, taking in the way Elisabeth was still glaring at the door; she had the feeling it would try to vanish again otherwise. Tucking his cane under his arm, he reached for the doorknob.

As soon as the door opened, Elisabeth understood what Silas had meant by *certain challenges*. The room looked a great deal like a cramped version of the Royal Library's catalog room, with old wooden drawers stacked along the walls from floor to ceiling, but in this case most of the drawers hung partway open and askew. The warm, syrupy light pouring through a mullioned window flickered with the shadows of dozens of grimoires flapping chaotically through the air. After decades without supervision, they'd all gone completely feral: shredded pages littered the dusty floorboards, and as Elisabeth watched, two small grimoires descended upon a third and began to tear it apart.

"No!" she cried, hurtling inside to break up the fight. As she separated the three grimoires, fending off the flapping pages of the aggressors with her elbows, she noticed that each of the open drawers had a yellowed, peeling label listing a range of years: 1511–1515, 1516–1520, and so on.

"You're all right," she told the torn grimoire fluttering weakly in her cupped hands. "Don't worry. I'll mend you."

No wonder the escaped grimoires were squabbling with each other. The older ones would disagree with the changes written down in the younger ones; the younger ones would chafe against the antiquated opinions of their elders. The drawers weren't just meant to organize them, but to keep them separated from each other. Sorted chronologically, they would be filed with other grimoires they liked, or at least wouldn't try to rip apart.

"My god, I think that one's been eaten," Nathaniel said, staring at a sad little pile of leather and parchment in the corner. He had just entered, his cane tapping on the dusty floorboards.

As one the grimoires went still, swiveling in his direction. "You might want to duck," Elisabeth said, but her warning came too late. A barrage of inkwads had already gone flying around the room.

It swiftly became apparent that scouring the Thorn family records would be no easy task. Nathaniel had frozen all the grimoires with a spell—they hung immobilized in the air, surrounded by rippling outlines of emerald light—but they numbered in the dozens, and they were suffering from all kinds of different ailments. An infection of White Motley had spread through the population, which was unsurprising, since the magical mold flourished in warm, poorly ventilated spaces, and on top of that, most of the grimoires were missing pages, torn out from their decades of squabbling.

The neglect infuriated Elisabeth, but nevertheless, she had to admit she was having fun. She liked nothing better than being surrounded by books, and she kept learning new things about sorcerers, finding interesting bits in the grimoires and asking Nathaniel about them, such as, "Why did they reinforce the battlements and install a drawbridge in 1587?"

"We were probably in the middle of a feud," he replied, squinting at a grimoire as he turned it upside down, then right side up again; she guessed it was the grimoire she'd examined earlier, whose text appeared upside down no matter the angle. "Sorcerers used to lay siege to each other's houses when the families had disagreements—over marriages, politics, which third cousin should inherit the demon, that sort of thing. Sometimes it lasted for years. They'd animate statues, catapult meteors at each other . . . That's one reason why the Reforms gained so much public support. Everyone got tired of sorcerers waging war with each other across public streets."

"Then I suppose the cauldron of hot oil makes sense," Elisabeth said, frowning, as she scanned her own grimoire. "But what about the imported crocodiles?"

Nathaniel grinned, his teeth bright against his ink-smeared face. "Naturally, those were for the moat."

Elisabeth imagined Mercy whacking a crocodile with

a broom on her way across Thorn Manor's ancestral drawbridge. Then a tendril of unease wormed through her stomach. A moment later, she remembered why.

"Nathaniel, about Mercy . . ." She hesitated. It seemed ridiculous, but she had to ask. "Has Silas ever killed a servant before?"

Nathaniel winced. Slowly, he lowered the grimoire in his hands. "Apparently, servants used to disappear from time to time under suspicious circumstances. A butler named Higgins went missing when I was eight or so; I overheard my parents discussing what might have happened to him one night when I was supposed to be in bed. Granted, it might not have been Silas. There are plenty of things that can happen to people in a city like Brassbridge."

"But you think it was him."

"Ah, well. According to my parents, Higgins was notorious for leaving fingerprints on the silver."

Elisabeth swallowed. She thought of Mercy working in a grand house for the first time, shouldering dozens of new responsibilities without proper training. Had she taken the job willingly? Perhaps she'd had no other choice. Elisabeth hadn't thought of that before, but in believing she was helping Mercy, she might have been trapping the girl in a life she didn't want.

Nathaniel was watching her. "Silas won't harm Mercy, I promise. He's just being dramatic about things not being done around the house exactly the way he likes."

"Then why did you order him not to kill her?" Elisabeth knew for a fact that Nathaniel was morally opposed to giving Silas orders. She had only seen him do it once, and it had clearly been a rare exception.

His eyes rested on her intently, a clear gray in the amber light. The window's diamond-shaped panes cast a pattern of shadows across his face. It occurred to her for the first time to wonder where the sunlight came from; they should be in an interior section of the house with no windows, and in all the hours they'd been inside, the quality of the light had never changed, suspended in a perpetual golden hour. At last Nathaniel said, "I trust him unreservedly. I would place my life in his hands without a moment's thought. I do, on a daily basis, every time he ties my cravat. But even though I don't believe he would harm a member of this household, I wasn't about to weigh my trust in him against Mercy's life. Silas understands that."

And he might even approve, Elisabeth thought. She still didn't fully grasp the strange dance that went on between them, the delicate balance they maintained between danger and understanding. Perhaps she never would. No matter how much she trusted Silas, she would never do so with the same complexity as Nathaniel, who had seen the demon kill his own father—and afterward, had immediately summoned him back.

Curiosity, more than anything, compelled her to ask, "Has he ever disobeyed an order?"

"Only once. It was wretched."

"What happened?"

Nathaniel shook his head. At first she thought that meant he wasn't going to answer, but then he started to speak, his face turned away, examining the crooked drawers. "I was twelve, and I grew angry with him . . . I can't remember why. Perhaps because he was acting too much like my mother or father, and it was them I really wanted. In any case, I ordered him to leave my room and forbade him from coming back. And then I stayed inside and wouldn't come out, not even to eat." A humorless smile plucked at the corner of his mouth.

"It was my first lesson in the specificity of orders. Previously, I hadn't understood how sorcerers could get killed by their own demonic servants. I hadn't considered the loopholes. I had ordered him to stay out of the room, but I hadn't ordered him not to open the door. Or put food inside, or knock, or speak to me from the hall. For days, we continued that game—he kept figuring out new ways to thwart me, and I kept giving him stricter and stricter orders. I remember barely being able to speak at the end; I must have been nearly dying of thirst. Eventually, he disobeyed. That's supposed to be impossible for demons—to defy a direct order—but he did it anyway." Nathaniel went quiet for a moment. "I thought he was going to die. Truly die, not just get sent back to the Otherworld. I resolved then that I would never give him another order unless I had no other choice. I haven't always kept that promise, but I can count on one hand the number of times I've slipped."

Elisabeth set down the grimoire she was holding, scooted over, and laid her head on his shoulder. Only afterward was she seized by the self-conscious fear that her touch might be unwelcome—that he might prefer to be left alone. But his hand came up and settled against the back of her head, his fingers threading through her hair.

Absently stroking, he continued quietly, "I still recall having the realization that if Silas had wanted to kill me, he could have done so a hundred times over. The orders I'd given him after summoning him, the ones I had assumed were protecting me from him all that time, had been a joke. They had been nothing to him at all."

Silence reigned in the muniment room. Around them the grimoires hung suspended, their pages softly whispering. She shifted to look up at Nathaniel.

The smudges of ink emphasized the contrast between his pale skin and the dark, silver-shot hair falling around his face. His gray eyes were slightly red-rimmed, his lips even redder, chapped by the winter cold. It was rare to see him look so serious. Guiltily, she thought it made him look almost too beautiful to bear.

She wished she could kiss him. She hated that she couldn't kiss him. The longing was an ache in her throat, a clenched yearning in her stomach, a desire that was somehow as sweet as it was painful. In that moment she thought fiercely that she would protect him from anything; she would battle villains, demons, monsters, to keep him safe. If she could, she would even battle his memories.

"Of course," he said suddenly. She lifted her head as he struggled upright, leaning on his cane. His eyes had lit with understanding. He stepped between the floating grimoires, rummaging around in his pocket. "These grimoires were all created by Thorns. The family connection should allow me to control them."

"How?" she asked, trying to stave off a nebulous sense of foreboding. He had produced a penknife from his pocket and was casually inspecting its edge.

"Oh, nothing complicated. Just some minor blood magic."

Elisabeth's hair nearly stood on end. "Isn't that illegal?"

He smiled down at her wickedly—the same smile that had once convinced her he abducted virgins and turned innocent girls into salamanders. "Not if it's your own blood," he said, and nicked his arm with the blade.

A thin red ribbon twined down his arm. Droplets of blood pattered onto the floorboards. Standing over them, he uttered a few sizzling words in Enochian, and the droplets hissed and steamed, evaporating.

A rustle ran through the frozen grimoires; an infiltrating tendril of emerald magic snaked between them. Then they began to spin, trapped in a glowing green whirlwind whose force tore at Elisabeth's hair and blew the dust from the floor and cabinets. Loose pages whipped around, sorting themselves into order, before snapping neatly back between their owners' covers. The drawers along the walls slid the rest of the way open in a drumming of muffled thumps and slams, and the grimoires poured into them, filling them up in orderly ranks.

Elisabeth stared openmouthed, thinking how useful it would be to have this spell in a Great Library. Katrien would love to see it. Then again, she might not be as captivated as Elisabeth was by the sight of Nathaniel at the height of his power, surrounded by the glow of sorcery, his hair and shirt whipped by an unearthly wind.

As the drawers finished shuffling closed, only one grimoire remained loose overhead, still eddying from the force of the dissipating whirlwind. Once it stopped twirling, it gently began to descend.

"I had better take it," Elisabeth volunteered, scrambling to her feet. "It looks like it's in bad shape."

That turned out to be an understatement. Only her long history with grimoires prevented her from dropping the volume when it settled into her waiting hands. Its cover was fuzzy with blotches of greenish-white mold, and it smelled strongly of curdled milk. Gingerly turning it over, she froze. "You won't believe who wrote this."

"Baltasar?"

"Worse," she declared. She reversed the grimoire so he could see the name blazoned across its spine:

CLOTHILDE THORN

FOUR

ELISABETH ISOLATED HERSELF in the south parlor the next day, surrounded by jars of unguents, tonics, and powders. White Motley was at its most contagious during treatment, when the fungus dried and started releasing spores, at which point the afflicted grimoire couldn't be allowed anywhere near Nathaniel's study. She was proud of the progress she'd made with his collection: though he treated his grimoires well, they had inevitably deteriorated after years without a librarian's touch. A handful had grown too moody or depressed to open. One had been suffering from an undiagnosed allergy to the pigments in its neighbor's binding, which caused it to sneeze explosively, spraying globs of ink across the study, and another had developed an oozing sore from chafing against a rough spot on the shelf.

She still hadn't decided exactly what she wanted to do with her future, but after weeks of attending lessons in the Royal Library's conservation hall, she had found that she shared many viewpoints with conservators, the goggled, aproned librarians tasked with restoring aged grimoires and nursing ailing volumes back to health. Conservators often butted heads with wardens—they valued the welfare of grimoires above all else, while wardens could be overly militant in their duty of protecting human life from dangerous books. Half of the workshop's chatter centered around criticizing the containment methods the wardens had chosen for a new Class Six in the archives, or the way they had transferred a high-security grimoire from one library to another, completely ignoring the conservators' recommendations. As the wardens saw it, making a grimoire more comfortable wasn't worth even a minor increased risk that it might break free and harm a civilian.

Elisabeth had learned a good deal from the lessons, and after witnessing what she could do with grimoires, the department was desperate to keep her. Yet she guiltily knew she didn't want to join the conservators forever. She couldn't envision being shut away in a workshop for the rest of her life, smelling perpetually of Brittle-Spine ointment, never wielding a sword.

If only there were an option in the middle—a mix between a warden and a conservator. She felt, with a passion that tore at her, that she could make a real difference: that given the chance, she could find a way to protect both humans and books equally.

Do not forget that the Collegium, too, can change. It simply needs the right people to change it. That was what Mistress Wick—now Director Wick, following Marius's resignation—had told her two months ago.

She was still trying to figure out the answer. In the meantime, she had plenty of other things to worry about.

The grimoire finally released a cloud of glowing green spores, which were so toxic they would put anyone who inhaled them into an enchanted coma for days. Muffled in a borrowed pair of goggles and a chemical-treated scarf, Elisabeth decided not to test the theory that her magical resistance might grant her some immunity. There wasn't time—according to Silas, the Midwinter Ball was supposed to take place in only one week. And besides, she'd promised Katrien she wouldn't do any experiments without her.

As the splotches of mold retreated, the white crust flaked away like dandruff to reveal patches of lumpy, inflamed leather beneath, at last exposing a title: Volume XXVI. The grimoire had to be feeling better. Yet the curdled-milk smell remained, and no matter what Elisabeth tried, she couldn't get it to open.

She tried coaxing; she tried compliments; she even once, her face screwed up resolutely, tried giving it a massage. But Volume XXVI remained stubbornly shut, like a puckered mouth refusing a spoon.

She wasn't about to succumb to despair. No matter how frustrating the task, she had discovered something marvelous back in the muniment room: Aunt Clothilde had been a *sorceress*.

"The same aunt whose tapestry you keep trying to get rid of?" Mercy asked dubiously, watching Elisabeth carefully apply leather polish to Volume XXVI's cover, bent over Nathaniel's desk amid sheaves of paper and glinting bronze-and-glass instruments.

"My great-great-aunt, technically," he corrected, stirring a cauldron over the fire. "And I'm not trying to get rid of it—I'm trying to destroy it. She put a spell on it that won't let anyone remove it from the wall. I tried setting fire to it once, but as you might imagine—"

"How many lady sorcerers are there?" Elisabeth interrupted hastily, glancing at Silas, who was napping in cat form on the sofa.

"Not many. Male heirs nearly always inherit the family demon, which is ridiculous, I know. Given my mother's skill at tricking Maximilian into eating his vegetables, I suspect she would have been far better at managing a demon than most men in the council."

Elisabeth frowned thoughtfully at her polish-stained rag. Coming as she did from the isolated world of the Great Libraries, such customs still made little sense to her. Nathaniel had told her once that few people outside the Collegium even knew about the existence of female wardens, and most would be shocked by the idea of women wearing trousers and wielding swords.

The thought gave her a pang of sympathy for Volume XXVI's creator. Whatever else Clothilde Thorn had been, she had clearly been strong-willed, enough so to leave an impression of her personality on the grimoire. Life in a world that barely accepted her couldn't have been easy. Perhaps she would have turned out differently had she lived under better circumstances, surrounded by the influence of other sorceresses. Elisabeth couldn't imagine not having Director Irena to look up to or Katrien to conspire with.

Katrien would surely have an idea about how to handle Volume XXVI. Usually, she came over once or twice a week for dinner. But there was no way to reach her now. Elisabeth doubted they'd be able to get a message past the hedge, or even out the door, for that matter. Yesterday, after the blizzard's snow began to melt, they had received an unpleasant surprise: none of the manor's entrances and exits would budge. They couldn't so much as open a window.

Just in case, she asked Nathaniel, who tried scribbling a message and magicking it to the Great Library, only for the paper to reappear in the air a split second later and smack him across the face. Discouraged but not defeated, they followed Mercy to the foyer to watch her poke the front door's letter slot with a broom. Seeing the end get snapped off like a carrot, they hastily decided not to provoke the house further.

They retreated to the study for a conference, discussing their options in lowered voices, as though afraid the manor might overhear. At one point during the hushed conversation Nathaniel and Elisabeth accidentally leaned too close together, their faces almost touching, and a clump of wet snow fell hissing into the fireplace, pointedly filling the room with smoke.

"That's it," he said, leaping to his feet with a theatrical swirl of his dressing gown. "Scrivener, there's something I need to show you."

Curiously, she followed him to the rose room, a disused bedchamber tucked away in a remote, drafty corner of the house. Her curiosity intensified as she watched him drag a wooden crate out from under the bed. It was nailed shut and stamped "EVIDENCE."

She had a bad feeling even before he pried it open to reveal the scrying mirror nestled in a bed of straw, the edges of the blades nearest its frame glistening with frost. She took a step back, her heart pounding. "What's that doing here? I thought it had been destroyed."

"Destroying artifacts this powerful can have unintended consequences. The Magisterium found a way to neutralize its magic instead. Afterward, they gave it back to me—it's been in my family for generations, and

I think they felt bad that I'd lost my sorcery." He made a face. "They delivered it while you were at the Royal Library. I meant to tell you, but I had completely forgotten about it until now."

"So it doesn't work any longer?" She cautiously drew nearer, peering into the crate. Up close, she saw the fine cracks spiderwebbing across the mirror's surface. Scorch marks darkened its warped silver frame, as though it had been through a fire.

"It does, but at a fraction of its former power. It only has a range of about a mile, and it can only look through the mirrors of places where the viewer has been invited."

Elisabeth bit the inside of her cheek. That didn't seem so terrible. "So it might be able to reach the Royal Library." She reached for its handle, then hesitated, feeling the chill of its metal in the air against her fingertips. The Preceptors' Committee wouldn't be pleased if they found out about this. They wouldn't care one bit that the mirror had been rendered mostly harmless. If there was one thing she had learned from last year's events, however, it was that she couldn't live her life by the Collegium's rules.

Mustering her courage, she plucked the mirror from the crate. Together she and Nathaniel climbed onto the bed's floral coverlet, leaning over it. Even damaged, its silver frame winked innocently, looking for all the world like it belonged on a lady's lace-trimmed vanity. But she couldn't forget the evil for which its twin had been used in Ashcroft's hands.

From a great distance, Director Wick's voice echoed back to her: *Knowledge always has the potential to be dangerous . . .*

Uncertain why, she glanced to Silas, who was lighting the lamps, his colorless hair limned by an unearthly white glow as he lowered a glass shade back into place. He met her eyes and gave the slightest nod.

Only then did she bend down and exhale across the mirror, watching her breath turn to frost. Then she lifted its icy handle, holding it so Nathaniel could see. This time of day, Katrien was likely to be in her room. The magic took a torturous moment to resolve.

As the fog cleared, an image swam into view. It was Katrien's chambers in the Royal Library, seen from the angle of the mirror above her dresser, but disappointingly, she was nowhere in evidence. A different familiar figure filled the frame, squinting at the papers spread out over her bed.

"Parsifal?" Elisabeth asked in surprise.

Parsifal jumped. "Elisabeth? Are you using a *scrying mirror*? Ah, hullo, Magister Thorn," he added, his ears turning pink.

Suddenly, the back of Katrien's head rose into view. She must have been sitting beside the dresser out of sight. "Don't speak, Parsifal," she said, draping a blanket over him. "This conversation is strictly confidential."

"I can still hear you," he said from beneath the blanket.

Katrien ignored him. Though Elisabeth hadn't called on her this way since Ashcroft, she didn't look remotely caught off guard by the intrusion when she turned around. "What trouble have you gotten yourselves into this time? I'm guessing it has something to do with the giant magical cyclone surrounding Nathaniel's house."

Nathaniel groaned. "I take it the entire city knows by now."

"Director Wick has been taking us on field trips. Don't make that face. Your wards are a superb example of the hazards of pre-Reforms sorcery."

Once Nathaniel was done sputtering, they explained everything that had happened with the wards so far. Elisabeth would have been more embarrassed to explain the kissing parts if she hadn't known that to Katrien, kissing was a purely scientific affair, like the mating habits of endangered beetles. While they spoke, her overlarge spectacles kept drifting down her nose, and she kept pushing them back up with her index finger.

"Won't the Collegium give you glasses that fit?" Nathaniel asked at last in frustration.

"These don't fit on purpose."

"What?"

"It's distracting," Katrien said. "You wouldn't believe what people will tell you when they're too busy being annoyed by your ill-fitting spectacles to pay attention to what you're saying. Anyway, I have an idea. Do you still own any of Clothilde's old belongings? Objects she was strongly attached to. The grimoire might cooperate in the presence of something familiar."

Elisabeth sat up straighter. "That's brilliant. She used to use the scrying mirror to spy on her in-laws, didn't she? Here . . ." She reached for Volume XXVI and brought it closer.

They held their breath for a moment, but nothing happened. The grimoire was asleep, making faint whistling noises, which cut off with a loud, disgruntled snort when Elisabeth hopefully attempted to pry it open.

"My theory's still sound," Katrien said. "Chances are she didn't have a personal attachment to the mirror. You'd be better off with something that she was in close contact with for long periods of time, like clothes or jewelry, or an object of emotional importance—a memento of some kind."

"The portrait!" Elisabeth was already charging out the door with the grimoire clasped against her chest. She returned a few minutes later, her heart galloping and her hair tousled from pelting down the attic stairs. "Didn't work!" she gasped. While she'd been up there, she was fairly sure one of the cursed dolls had moved.

"Strange that she wasn't attached to it," Nathaniel mused. "I thought it captured her warts at a remarkably flattering angle. Silas," he added, twisting around, "you served Clothilde back in the day." Elisabeth found this shockingly difficult to imagine. "Does she still have a bedroom around here somewhere?"

Silas paused. "In this matter, master, I am afraid I cannot help you."

"Why? Did she order you not to tamper with her things before she died?"

"No," he replied.

"Then what is it?"

Just then, the door creaked open. Mercy had warily poked her head into the study. Silas didn't acknowledge her arrival. He had gone perfectly still, his narrow back rigid.

At last his cold, soft voice broke the silence. "Her wardrobe, Master Thorn. I shall not go near it. It is a stain upon your house. Never before or since have I beheld garments so disgracefully out of fashion." With that, he turned and left the room, sweeping past Mercy like a frigid draft.

She stared after him, incredulous. She looked to Elisabeth and Nathaniel for an explanation. That was all it took; they both dissolved into hysterics. They clutched each other to keep from doubling over, red-faced and shaking with laughter. The scrying mirror tumbled from Elisabeth's grip onto the bedspread, taking Katrien's narrowed eyes with it.

"At least we know Clothilde still has a room in the manor," Nathaniel choked out.

"Let's find it," Elisabeth wheezed, breathless. "We have to—we have to see it!"

"The knowledge is forbidden, mistress," he replied, in such an accurate impression of Silas's whisper that she collapsed onto her side, howling.

"Can I take the blanket off now?" asked Parsifal.

Elisabeth could have spent the rest of her life exploring Thorn Manor's hidden rooms. Over the next few days, wandering up and down the hallways and glaring sternly at the walls, she discovered over a dozen secret chambers. Some of these, she gave names: the blue room, the jasmine room, the orchid room. Most were bedrooms, but she also found a few parlors and studies, and a small, ancient kitchen that Nathaniel thought had probably been magicked away to avoid the effort of a renovation. Once she even stumbled across an old-fashioned water closet that looked like it belonged inside a castle, with a grimy scalloped window and a wooden bench that had a hole cut in it for the toilet seat.

"I'd rather not know why someone felt the need to

hide this one for eternity," Nathaniel commented, shutting the door before she could barge inside.

No matter how many rooms Elisabeth found, she couldn't help returning again to one in particular. For reasons she couldn't explain, she liked to go there alone. It was located in a sunny nook beside a staircase on the third floor. The door always materialized of its own volition at her approach, as though shyly pleased she kept wanting to visit.

She called it the ostrich room. It had a welcoming atmosphere, with its bright south-facing window and peeling pink wallpaper. A layer of dust coated everything, including the real stuffed ostrich standing in one corner. She suspected that the room had belonged to a lady sorcerer; a glimmer of old magic seemed to hang in the air, as delicate and faded as the wallpaper. Sometimes, passing the armoire or inspecting the tiny glass bottles on the vanity, she caught a faint whiff of a woman's perfume, as though its owner had only just walked out the door.

This time, inspecting the desk by the window, she found a beautiful hand-calligraphed opera ticket dating back to 1712. As she peered at it, trying to puzzle out the name of the opera, Silas's whispering voice spoke behind her.

"This room has not been opened in a hundred years, mistress."

She jumped and guiltily turned around. She had no idea how long Silas had been standing there watching her. But it turned out he wasn't watching her after all: he stood gazing at a rose-colored gown on a wire stand, which she hadn't noticed before amid the clutter.

As she grasped uselessly for words, he spoke again without turning. "If you look closely out the window, you will see that the view is identical to that of the solar. It is the same angle, even though this room is on the third floor, and the solar on the second."

Feeling oddly flustered, as though she had intruded on a private moment, Elisabeth hurriedly brought her face to the clouded glass. A layer of ice glazed the window, creating lacy patterns of frost on the diamond-shaped panes. But even with the view partially obscured, she saw that he was right: she could just make out the garden's ice-encrusted fountain. It was as though this room and the solar were somehow sharing the same space in the manor.

Something else about the view struck her as peculiar. After a moment she realized that the winter day outside couldn't possibly belong to the present time. There was no debris whirling past, and the carriage parked on the other side of the placid, well-trimmed hedge looked decidedly antique.

Her head hurt thinking about it. What would happen if guests were sitting in the solar right now, or at this exact time in the room's frozen past? If she stood quietly enough, would she be able to hear a ghost of their conversation and laughter, taste the faded sparkle of their champagne?

She thought of the vanity's perfume, and couldn't help an involuntary shiver. In response, a chest's lid creaked behind her. Then a blanket settled around her shoulders, soft and smelling of cedar. She turned, holding the blanket close, as Silas stepped away. His movements had barely stirred the dust motes in the air.

"Why would people want to hide these rooms if it isn't to save space?" she asked.

"Sorcerers often keep secrets. Some of the occupants hoped to prevent their descendants from going through their belongings." He carefully lifted the opera ticket from the desk between two gloved fingers. "Others simply wished to be forgotten."

She was about to ask why anyone would want that. But then she saw the way Silas was studying the ticket, gazing inscrutably into the past, and felt the weight of history in the room sift down upon her like a fine golden dust, filling up her lungs. She remembered the little girl's empty bedroom in the dollhouse grimoire, and felt the same muffling silence descend.

"Did you care about her?" she asked quietly. "The woman who lived here?"

"Not in a way you might understand." Nevertheless, after a pause, he slipped the ticket into an inner pocket of his jacket. She understood how much he was deliberately revealing in letting her see him do it— perhaps more than he would reveal to Nathaniel.

Elisabeth hesitated. She had to ask, even if a part of her didn't want to know the answer. "Silas . . . is it true about the servants?"

The question didn't take him by surprise. He only bowed a little, as though inviting her judgment. "I have served the Thorn family for over three hundred years. In that time, I have seen many servants come and go.

Some were not of a character I deemed suitable. There have been murderers. Thieves. There have been men like those who chased you into the alley. Let us say I hastened their decision to resign."

She swallowed. "What about Higgins? What did he do?"

"Ah." Silas glanced at her from beneath his lashes. "I'm afraid he was one of the worst of all. He left fingerprints on the silver."

She sat down heavily on the vanity's stool. "I can never tell if you're joking."

"Just as well, perhaps," he said, reaching to tuck the blanket back into place; it had slipped from her shoulder.

"I know you wouldn't hurt Mercy."

He tilted his head ambiguously—neither a yes nor a no.

"You wouldn't."

"I would not," he agreed, "but not because I am good." Though he sounded almost sympathetic, his eyes held no warmth. Behind them stretched a twisting labyrinth of years, of ancient thoughts and motives beyond guessing. "As a demon, I am incapable of remorse. If a human inconveniences me, my instinct is to dispose of them. I would not feel guilt if I killed Mercy, just as I have never felt guilt over the many other humans I have killed, some of them innocents, even children. In fact, I would enjoy it. I know you do not wish to believe this of me, but you must."

Reflexively, she drew the blanket closer around her body. "That can't be true. I've seen . . ."

"Regret," he said softly. "I do feel regret, mistress."

The window's chill crept over her hair and exposed skin. She recalled what he had said to her last autumn: *There is no absolution for a creature such as I.*

"After I summoned you, I thought"—she hesitated—"*hoped* that you might have undergone a . . . a transformation, that you might no longer be a demon, or no longer crave human life, but if that isn't true . . ."

"I'm afraid such a thing is not possible."

She wrestled back the question desperate to leap forth: *Do you wish it were?* She suspected she already knew the answer, even though no sign of it showed on his face, his fine-boned features as remote as a marble carving. After a moment of silent turmoil, she reached out to clasp his hand. "I told Nathaniel once that I might not have seen what he can do, but I've seen what he chooses to do. You may not be good by nature—"

"Mistress Scrivener," he cautioned.

"But you've made your choice," she finished, searching his face. "I know you have. To be Silas, not Silariathas."

He didn't deny it. The very fact that she had spoken his old name aloud, and nothing had happened—that its syllables hadn't stung her ears, that her voice hadn't echoed with its terrible power—was proof enough alone. His hand twitched as though he might retract it from her grip, but he stilled himself, his yellow eyes unfathomable.

There were so many things she wanted to say to him, their unspoken magnitude crowding her throat. That it seemed to her there were different ways to be good; that it was easier for a man to act like a monster than a monster to act like a man. But for him it would be like hearing reassurances from a child. The silence spun out for a long minute, and she eventually realized, seeing the way Silas gazed past her, through her, as though he had forgotten the mortal passage of time, that she would have to be the one to end it.

"Now you're supposed to give me an ominous warning," she prompted.

He blinked, coming back to himself, and regarded her evenly. "It seems they do not work on you, mistress, which I find deeply vexing."

Elisabeth laughed, but Silas didn't look offended. Rather, he seemed gratified to have amused her, or perhaps—and she had to admit this was equally likely—relieved that her probing into his private affairs had ended.

She paused, turning over her next words. She couldn't let the opportunity pass by. She was responsible for bringing Mercy into the household, and merely ensuring the girl's survival wasn't enough. Mercy deserved to be happy.

"You may ask anything of me," he remarked, her thoughts as transparent to him as ever. "I will obey as though I am bound by your command."

Roused from her contemplation, Elisabeth bristled. "I don't want that. If you agree to something I ask, it has to be of your own free will. As an equal, not a servant."

A smile touched his face, and she realized the irony of her demand. Though demons might playact at being servants, they considered their human masters little more than insects to be toyed with, inferior in every respect. But he only said, "I assure you, there is nothing you could ask of me that I would find objectionable."

She scowled at him.

"Very well. I will be kind to Mercy—for my own sake, for I do not wish to see you unhappy."

With that, he bent and drew her fingers to his lips. A kiss grazed her knuckles so softly that she might have imagined it; it might have been only his breath she felt against her skin. Then he was gone, leaving her alone in the room with the dust motes and the sun streaming onto the faded wallpaper.

FIVE

THEY MADE A breakthrough the next morning during breakfast. They were eating sleepily, Elisabeth browsing last Monday's morning paper (one of the articles had been cut out, leaving a rectangular hole behind; she suspected it of being related to the Midwinter Ball), when Nathaniel flung down a slice of bacon hard enough to rattle the cutlery. "Of course!" he exclaimed. "The tapestry!" Without explanation, he leaped to his feet and dashed from the room.

As Silas sighed, lifting Nathaniel's fallen napkin from the floor, Elisabeth eyed the abandoned bacon with interest. Once she had gulped it down, she took Nathaniel's half-empty plate and scraped the leftover eggs into her mouth for good measure. Then, chewing vigorously, she thundered after him, leaving Mercy sitting baffled at the table.

It didn't take her long to determine where Nathaniel had gone. She could hear his cane rapping smartly on the floor, traveling down the hallway behind the scullery.

She could count on one hand the number of times she had ventured down that hall. Her memory supplied murky images of a gloomy corridor with outdated furniture lurking dismally in the shadows, their shapes readily mistakable for hunched-over imps and goblins.

She retrieved Demonslayer from the foyer ("No swords at the breakfast table, mistress," Silas had ruled) and then hurried after the sound of Nathaniel's fading steps.

The hallway was as bad as she remembered. Pallid light struggled through the cracks between the drawn curtains, trickling claustrophobically over dark wood paneling and scratched, dusty floorboards. The sagging brocade armchairs clustered along the walls looked like they were huddling together for warmth.

When she caught up with Nathaniel, she crowded closer to his back than strictly necessary. "What are you doing?" she asked.

He snapped his fingers, and green flames blazed to life in the cobweb-draped sconces, illuminating the offensive mauve expanse of Aunt Clothilde's tapestry, which depicted a cloying scene of a princess attended by a unicorn and a tame lion. Whoever had made it wasn't a very good artist, in Elisabeth's opinion; it had the same problem as some of Thorn Manor's gargoyles, which was that the lion's face looked unsettlingly like a human's.

"It's obvious, isn't it? Her room must be hidden behind this appalling tapestry." He swept the tapestry aside with a dramatic flourish.

Nothing happened, except for a good deal of dust, which made Elisabeth sneeze. Narrowing his eyes, Nathaniel muttered an incantation. Not much more happened this time—just an anticlimactic green fizzle and a whiff of aetherial combustion.

"Let me try," she said hastily, before the hallway could begin to smell like one of Katrien's experiments. She squared her shoulders and faced the wall assertively. "May we please enter?"

A door's outline grudgingly wavered into view, barely distinguishable from the dusty molding. Then it started to fade again, in a rather surly fashion, as though it hoped they would give up and leave.

"She'll kick you down if you don't let her in," Nathaniel advised, and the door reappeared again in a hurry.

"Don't be rude," Elisabeth warned under her breath.

"Scrivener, you cannot deny that the house started it."

Shaking her head, she reached for the doorknob. Before she turned it, she took a fortifying breath. Even though she knew ghosts didn't exist, it seemed possible that the vengeful spirit of Aunt Clothilde might come swooping out at them, wattles and all.

The door swung open on a woman's bedroom bathed in an eerie, flickering pink light. Everything was trimmed in sagging lace—the bed skirt, the curtains, the tablecloth over the nightstand. Tiptoeing inside, Elisabeth felt her skin crawl. Rosy flames danced low in the hearth, as though someone had just been inside tending the fire.

"Enchanted flames," Nathaniel explained. "They don't emit heat, but the spell can last for ages. Brassbridge's streetlamps used to be lit with them prior to the invention of gaslight."

Elisabeth realized she was clenching Demonslayer's

hilt and loosened her grip. She glanced around more curiously, her eyes lingering on a mirrored tray covered in small porcelain figurines. She experimentally touched a box on the nightstand, which sprang open unexpectedly, filling the room with a tinkling out-of-tune melody as a faded model ballerina twirled around inside, moving in agonized fits and jerks.

She hastily clapped it shut.

A hulking baroque wardrobe occupied the wall across from the bed. A thrill of mingled excitement and trepidation ran through her, but when Nathaniel tested the doors, they remained firmly shut. "Locked. Do you see any hairpins?"

After she retrieved some from the vanity, mystified, he bent to fiddle with the lock. She found the sight of his long, pale fingers manipulating the hairpins peculiarly entrancing. With his silver-shot hair falling over his face in concentration, he explained, "Silas taught me how to pick locks in between lessons about which spoon to use for soup and how to make conversation at a dinner party. He claims that sorcerers would be better off if they learned to be more practical, instead of relying on magic for everything . . ."

"I can't imagine why," Elisabeth said.

"Yes, he's clearly delusional." Surveying his handiwork, Nathaniel made a face. "This might take a while. I'm out of practice."

The dimness couldn't help. She went over to wrench open the curtains, letting in a flood of light that billowed with particles of dust. It spilled across a collection of books on the lace-shrouded sideboard, their covers littered with shriveled petals fallen from a vase. They were ordinary books, not grimoires, bearing such titles as *Modern Etiquette and Propriety* and *A Manual of Proper Comportment for Ladies*. Scattered among them were yellowed leaflets that Elisabeth eventually determined to be outraged moral treatises about young women wearing immodest clothing and straying from their natural role in the home.

Her remaining sympathy for Clothilde evaporated.

Behind her, Nathaniel made a choking sound. She whirled around in alarm. But he wasn't hurt; his shoulders were shaking with laughter. He had gotten Clothilde's wardrobe open and removed—something. At first it appeared to be a dead animal's pelt, until she noticed it had tassels. A dressing gown?

As she stared in horrified fascination, he swept it around his shoulders as though he were donning his magister's cloak. Then he struck a pose, his eyes sparkling with mischief over the ratty fur fringe. "How do I look?"

Elisabeth couldn't answer. She was having the complicated realization that she still wanted to kiss Nathaniel even while he was wearing an old lady's hideous dressing gown.

He grinned at her villainously, then dove back into the wardrobe, rummaging through an age-brittled froth of lace and chiffon. He reemerged with a dress and held it up in invitation. It was the same mauve hue as the tapestry outside, with an oppressive floral print and a distinct air of being haunted by the set of curtains butchered to create it. Ruffles cascaded down the sleeves. Elisabeth thought it might be the most nightmarish thing she had ever seen, even after Mr. Hob.

"No," she said emphatically.

"Come on."

Mutely, she shook her head.

"I've seen you fight demons, Scrivener."

Elisabeth took a step back. "That dress belongs in the Hall of Forbidden Arts."

"But imagine the look on Silas's face. If you won't try it on, I'm afraid I'll have no choice but to do it myself. It wouldn't be the first time Silas has seen me in a dress. In fact, it might not even be the second . . ."

Nathaniel continued talking, but Elisabeth had stopped listening in favor of scrutinizing one of the dressing gown's loose-hanging sleeves. She had thought she'd seen it twitch. Surely it was just her imagination.

But then the sleeve lifted into the air, as though an invisible arm had snuck inside, controlling it like a puppeteer. At once, she remembered the suit of armor in the attic. "Watch out!" she shouted.

Her warning came too late. The dressing gown's other sleeve flew up, and together they engulfed him in a flurry of battering tassels. She started forward just as a blast of emerald flame sent the garment flying across the room, where it smacked against the wall and limply slid to the floor. Nathaniel was left disheveled and panting, his collar open, green sparks of magic still dancing over his skin. He met her eyes and let out an astonished laugh, looking rather debauched.

By Aunt Clothilde's dressing gown, she tried not to think.

Acting swiftly, she yanked the mauve dress from his hands and shoved it into the wardrobe, and not a moment too soon; the moment she slammed the doors shut, the wardrobe began to judder aggressively.

Their eyes went to the dressing gown. For a moment, the puddle of fabric appeared defeated. Then it lifted from the carpet as though raised by a theater wire, its arms dangling limply at its sides and its long, crooked shadow stretching toward them across the ceiling.

They looked at each other. "Run," they said in unison.

They got partway down the hall before Clothilde's door slammed wide open against the wall with a crack like a gunshot, and a furious tide of clothing came boiling out. A garish assortment of hats, stockings, gowns, shifts, knickers, and corsets tumbled through the air after them as though blown by an enormous gust of wind.

Mercy skidded into view at the end of the hallway. Her face hardened at the sight of the approaching forces. Bravely, she raised her mop.

"Mercy, run!" Elisabeth bellowed.

"No, save us!" Nathaniel yelled.

Mercy went a shade paler. "Are those bloomers?" she shouted.

Elisabeth risked a glance over her shoulder, only to find a great pair of ancient bloomers almost upon them, rippling angrily as they descended. She let out a ferocious roar. Demonslayer's blade flashed, shredding the fabric to ribbons. The pieces fluttered to the carpet and didn't rise again, a sight that reassured her until her eyes fell on the remainder of the army: clothes still streamed from Clothilde's open door, their numbers seemingly inexhaustible.

A fizzling crack split the air as Nathaniel summoned his fiery green whip. It licked out, glaringly bright, illuminating the dim hall like a flash of lightning. When it coiled back to his side, the garments at the vanguard had been reduced to a smoking heap. And not just that: a long horizontal gash ran along the wall, the edges of the wallpaper smoldering. After a defeated pause, one of the armchairs toppled over, sliced in two.

"Possibly not the best weapon for close quarters," he admitted. "Though frankly, that chair did need to be put out of its misery."

Elisabeth was beginning to understand Silas's frequent references to Nathaniel setting himself on fire. Perhaps he had the same thought, because the whip fizzled out of existence. The remainder of the clothes, lurking warily out of range, immediately surged forward.

They set off again, Elisabeth throwing Nathaniel's arm over her shoulder when his knee gave out. "We'll have to make a stand in the foyer," he panted, hopping along on his good leg. "We need reinforcements."

Mercy shot him a skeptical look. "From who?"

Elisabeth shared her doubts. If Silas meant to help them, he would have made an appearance by now. She imagined him sitting in the solar, calmly reading a newspaper while ignoring the sounds of mayhem below. And if not Silas, who else could Nathaniel mean?

Annoyingly, he just grinned. "You'll see."

They reached the foyer in the nick of time. Elisabeth and Mercy closed ranks around Nathaniel, battling back the clothes as he bent his head to recite an incantation. Whatever magic he was working, it had to be significant. Energy built in the room as though a thunderstorm were brewing, making Elisabeth's ears pop and the fine hairs stand up on the back of her neck. The feel of it reminded her a little of when he'd brought the Royal Library's statues to life, but she wasn't able to ruminate on that for long; an attacking frock required her full attention.

Mercy's mop proved surprisingly effective as a weapon. After it had smacked a garment to the floor, the sopping-wet fabric was too heavy to do much more than flop around. But the mop was unwieldy, and Mercy could only target one piece of clothing at a time. Soon the clothes grew wise to her tactics. A pair of hosiery wrapped themselves around the mophead, entangling it and making it even clumsier.

Sweat beaded Elisabeth's brow. A ruffled blouse nearly broke through her defenses. A straw hat bounced off her face, its feather plume quivering indignantly, followed by a lacy brassiere.

"How much longer is this spell going to take?" she yelled.

Nathaniel lifted his head, a curl of dark hair loose over his forehead, his expression positively demonic. A raucous screeching and squawking answered from the top of the stairs, followed by a muffled pounding like a dozen rugs being beaten at once. Then a great flock of peacocks, nightingales, and birds of paradise came pouring down the stairway into the foyer in a chaos of beating wings. Their iridescent feathers flashed in jeweled glimmers as they tore into the clothes with their beaks and claws. Stunned, Elisabeth recognized them as belonging to the rather busy bird-patterned wallpaper in the green room.

Her wits returned quickly. Living with Nathaniel, this sort of thing was more or less in line with a regular Tuesday. She pressed the advantage, slicing down an embroidered chemise that had managed to slip through a peacock's grasp.

"Where is the dressing gown?" Nathaniel shouted into her ear, looking like he was having more fun than a person had any right to be defending himself against his great-great-aunt's homicidal knickers. "We need to find it while the rest are distracted!"

"We need to what?" she shouted back, barely able to hear him through the birds' cacophonous shrieking.

"The dressing gown is the spell's anchor!" he yelled, enunciating each word. "If we defeat it, the others will stop trying to murder us!"

Elisabeth's heart leaped. She cast around. There— lurking behind a frilly coat, a flash of mustard-colored tassels.

She knew exactly how to lure it out of hiding. "Kiss me," she said grimly.

Nathaniel's eyebrows rose. "Elisabeth," he shouted loudly enough for the entire manor to hear, "I knew your tastes were unconventional, but I had no idea you found this sort of thing so stimulating. If you'd like, we could save a few outfits for—"

He wasn't able to finish, because she seized his face and kissed him. Tearing away from his delighted laugh, Mercy's face blazing red at the periphery of her vision, Elisabeth felt her embarrassment give way to a fierce clench of triumph when she saw that the dressing gown had strayed out into the open, its tassels trembling in fury. Letting out a victorious shout, she barreled through the melee. The gown saw her coming: it shot evasively toward the kitchen, but before it could escape, she seized it by the hem and tackled it to the floor. Supposing iron might work as well on evil pajamas as it did on demons, she plunged Demonslayer through its ruffled waist.

Ballooning with air, the dressing gown sank gently to the marble tiles. It gave one last feeble twitch, and didn't rise again.

Elisabeth's ears popped. Then the rest of the clothing went lifeless, raining down across the foyer in a soft patter. Shaking off a stocking, she found that the room now resembled the scene of an elaborate prank. Clothes hung limply over the banister and dangled from the chandelier; one particularly disturbing pair of gauzy underwear festooned the front door's doorknob. The remaining birds swept back up the stairwell, their loud cries fading into rustling sounds as they transformed back into paper.

Surveying the mess (and, Elisabeth suspected, staunchly avoiding their eyes), Mercy rolled up her sleeves. "Suppose we'd better get this cleaned up before . . ."

She trailed off. Silas had appeared in the shadows, gazing across the foyer at the dressing gown as though beholding the corpse of an ancient nemesis, his face devoid of expression save for his haunted yellow eyes.

Hastily, Elisabeth said, "I'll go get the grimoire."

"Do you mean," she asked several hours later, loitering nosily in the hall, "that the house wants Nathaniel to declare his intentions?"

Silas stood before the door to Nathaniel's study, his

polite knock having gone unanswered a second time. In
his gloved hand, he held a small brown bottle contain-
ing one of Dr. Godfrey's tinctures. Elisabeth kept giving
him surreptitious glances, but he seemed perfectly normal, his uniform spotless and his demeanor composed.
Earlier, by silent mutual agreement, they had left him
alone in the foyer. She had no idea what he had done
with Aunt Clothilde's clothes, and was honestly too
afraid to ask.

"It appears so, mistress," he replied.

She crouched to peer through the study's keyhole.
Volume XXIV had opened as soon as they'd brought
it to Clothilde's room, and Nathaniel had spent several
minutes studying the diagram of Clothilde's altered
ward, his expression growing increasingly appalled,
before sweeping back to his study, where he had
remained shut away for the past few hours. Clouds of
noxious purple smoke kept pouring out from the crack
beneath the door, joined on one occasion by a screeching flock of bats. The latter incident likely explained
why Mercy was clutching an umbrella.

Through the keyhole, Elisabeth could only see
a piece of Nathaniel's desk and the shelves behind it,

lined with grimoires. The velvet of Silas's uniform coat brushed against her cheek as he reached over her to open the door.

Nathaniel didn't acknowledge their entrance. He was pacing in front of the fire with a hitch in his stride that made her wince—his leg had to be hurting after their dash to the foyer. "I find it difficult to believe," he declared loudly to no one in particular, "that my house does not think I am properly committed. I cannot imagine a single thing I have ever done to give it that impression."

Silas shut his eyes. "You might begin by using Mistress Scrivener's given name, instead of eternally calling her 'Scrivener.'"

"What?" Nathaniel whirled around. "I don't do that."

"You did it twenty-seven times yesterday, master."

Nathaniel turned to Mercy, who shrugged in agreement.

Elisabeth braced herself for another explosion of bats. But Nathaniel only threw himself down on his favorite armchair to study Silas and Mercy in suspicion. "Are you two co-conspirators now? Are you plotting against me? How long has this been going on?"

Mercy squared her shoulders. "Silas had a talk with me this morning about how he isn't going to murder me and bury me in the back garden. He gave me his word as a gentleman."

"That's oddly specific," Nathaniel remarked. "Elisabeth, remind me to never dig up the petunias." He caught her eye and mouthed, "Higgins."

"What do we do next?" Elisabeth inquired hastily, before Mercy could start asking questions. "About the wards, I mean."

Nathaniel sent Silas a harrowed look that she didn't understand. Silas sighed, turning to her.

"It seems likely, mistress, that the manor will only be appeased by a show of formal courtship."

SIX

"BACK IN THE old days, sorcerous families had their own courtship traditions," Nathaniel explained later. "I only know about them from stories. No one's practiced them in centuries, especially after the Reforms."

"But the Reforms were meant to stop sorcerers' duels and human sacrifices, and that sort of thing," Elisabeth said, frowning as she pulled grimoires from the shelves.

"Exactly," Nathaniel replied. "According to my ancestors, nothing screams romance like a good old-fashioned duel to the death."

He was still in the armchair, though not necessarily by choice; he had tried standing up, only to slowly sink back down with his face drained of color. Exhibiting a pointed lack of surprise, Silas had made him put his foot up on a pillow and fed him a spoonful of Dr. Godfrey's tincture as though he were a child.

Elisabeth shot him worried glances as she clambered around the study's ladders, consulting various grimoires for more information about magical courtship. She wasn't certain whether this turn of events had left her nervous or excited. Her palms were sweaty, and her stomach kept flopping around like a fish trapped in a net. Whenever she caught Nathaniel looking back at her, her heart skipped a panicked beat. The novels she'd read had never mentioned that being in love had symptoms, like food poisoning or influenza.

At last she found a promising candidate in A Lady's Guide to Sorcerous Traditions by Dame Prudence Winthrop, which she suspected of being Aunt Clothilde's acquisition: it had a pink fabric cover and smelled of old, dried-up roses. She brought it down to the fire, thinking Nathaniel might have a better idea of what to look for, but it gave a loud, scandalized gasp when he tried to open it, clapping back shut in a waft of floral perfume.

"You might need to cover your eyes," Elisabeth told him apologetically, retrieving it from his hands. She settled on the rug with her back against the armchair, acutely aware that if she moved an inch or two to the side, she would be tucked against his good leg, able to lean her head against his knee.

Lady's Guide gave an indignant little huff at the treatment, but cheered considerably when Elisabeth told it she had a suitor—not even a lie, she realized, sneaking a glance at Nathaniel. He was reclining against one of the armrests with a hand draped long-sufferingly over his forehead, his pinkie and ring fingers lifted slightly, as though he were about to peek. But he didn't; she watched him for a moment, taking in his lowered lashes, dark against his pale cheeks, and the way the shadow cast by his hand cut through the sharp angle of his cheekbone. Then she turned back to the grimoire, her face hot.

Now that Nathaniel wasn't looking, Lady's Guide proved eager to share its confidence. Shivering in anticipation, it flipped to a relevant section and solicitously tucked a silk ribbon between the pages to mark the place. Elisabeth spent a few minutes puzzling out the writing, which used antiquated language like *He must shew you his ardor in a myriad of wayes*. Turning the pages, her frown deepened. She paused on an illustration of a sorcerer unleashing magic against a fire-breathing wyrm.

A chime of silver against porcelain heralded Silas's return with the tea. "How many sorcerers used to die while courting?" she asked, looking up.

"A significant percentage. I assure you, mistress, it was usually for the best." As he bent over her to place their teacups on the side table, she noted that Lady's Guide didn't react to his presence, even after his gaze flicked briefly toward its pages.

"When I die in pursuit of your favor, make sure the obituary mentions that it wasn't for my lack of razor-sharp wit and keenly honed reflexes." Nathaniel reached out, blindly groping for his tea, which he nearly spilled until Silas placed the cup in his hand.

Doing her best to ignore him, Elisabeth turned more pages. "Have you ever heard of the three impossible tasks?" she asked finally.

"A princess falls into an enchanted sleep, and the only way to break the curse is by moving a mountain or fetching her starlight in a jar—that sort of thing?"

"I thought you didn't read fairy tales," she said, surprised.

A rueful smile touched the corner of his mouth. "I said I didn't believe in them. I never said I hadn't read them."

Thoughtfully, she flipped back to an illustration of a sleeping princess clasping a rose. Looking at it sent a shiver of wonder through her, for the faded illustration moved: the princess's chest gently rose and fell beneath her embroidered gown, and petals drifted free one by one to settle beneath the dangling fingers of her other hand, which had slipped from her bed in slumber.

Slowly, she said, "There's all sorts of advice in here about a lady's suitors winning duels and slaying dragons on her behalf, or bestowing her with priceless magical treasures—which I don't want, by the way— but I've found something else that looks interesting."

"In a fairy tale?" His tone was carefully neutral.

She nodded. Her heart pounded shallowly and her fingertips tingled, as though she were teetering on the edge of a precipice. "It's called the Lovers' Pact. According to legend, a sorcerer who carries out three impossible tasks has the right to ask his true love's hand in marriage under any circumstances, even if the family objects or the king forbids their union. Nothing, not even magic, can tear them apart." She went on hastily, "Which might mean you don't have to do anything dangerous to appease the wards, necessarily."

"Just impossible. That's a relief."

To her desperate gratitude, he didn't seem to have noticed that she'd said the word "marriage." Silas certainly had; she felt the featherlight touch of his gaze upon her, even though by the time she looked, he was impassively tending the fire.

She swallowed. "In the story, didn't the boy who woke the princess bring her starlight by reflecting it in water? So the three tasks only have to seem like they *should* be impossible. Even if Aunt Clothilde objects, she'll be forced to obey tradition."

"Or," Nathaniel pointed out, "it's a fairy tale, not an ancient and binding magical law, and the wards won't care about it one way or the other."

"There's only one way to find out."

He sighed. "Three impossible tasks," he mused, absently tracing his index finger over the contours of his face, his eyes still closed. A long moment passed. "Well?" he asked finally.

Hope swelled in her chest. "Well what?"

"I imagine you have to set the tasks. Someone does."

She was glad that he couldn't see her expression. When Lady's Guide gave a tiny squeak of protest, she realized she was squeezing the grimoire and apologetically set it aside.

True love. She hadn't said so out loud, but the fairy tale was insistent about that being an essential part of the Lovers' Pact. If it was real in the first place—and, though she couldn't say why, she felt certain that it was—it would only work if she was Nathaniel's true love.

And if she wasn't . . .

He wouldn't know any better. He would think he was right about it just being a fairy tale, and they would try something else.

Squeezing her eyes shut, she drew her knees to her chest. As she had said earlier herself, there was only one way to find out. She needed to come up with the first impossible task.

Concentrating, she racked her brain for the most unlikely thing at which she could imagine Nathaniel succeeding—something that even the manor's wards would consider impossible to the extreme. And when at last an idea occurred to her, the thought was so alarming she could barely voice it out loud.

She slept in her own room that night, as she had ever since the incident with the roof. Or at least, she meant to—but sleep wouldn't find her. She tossed and turned, filled with a wild, restless energy, her mind racing in circles. Occasionally she kicked her legs around beneath the covers, but this failed to bring relief. Finally she threw the blankets aside in frustration. She went to the window and pressed her hot cheek against it, letting the icy glass chill her skin.

Before tonight, she hadn't truly felt trapped inside the manor. Now she would give anything to take a brisk walk through Hemlock Park, scouring her lungs with cold night air, cooling her fevered thoughts beneath the wintry glittering of the stars.

Every time she closed her eyes, she saw Nathaniel as he had looked that evening, the firelight tracing his angular features, his closed eyes shadowed beneath his hand.

Her heart ached. She knew that what she was feeling was love, being in love with him, but didn't understand why it felt this way—like being on a ship with land a distant green sliver on the horizon, the wind tearing at her hair, unsure whether she was casting off from shore into unknown waters, or whether she was finally returning home. She couldn't tell which, because it seemed like both at once. It was a feeling almost like madness.

She had never thought a great deal about what her future with Nathaniel might involve. Now she was unable to stop.

If the Lovers' Pact worked, would they end up marrying?

Did she *want* to get married?

She could hardly wrap her mind around the idea. She was only seventeen. If she and Nathaniel married, their life together would span far more years than she had even been alive. How many—fifty? Sixty? With the decades claimed by Silas's bargain returned to them, they might both live to their eighties. The enormity of those numbers seemed made-up, impossible to comprehend. Overwhelmed, she buried her forehead in the crook of her arm.

A terrible thought came to her then: after a life spent together, they would both die, but one of them would die first. One day, one of them would have to lose the other. That was what it meant to love.

Suddenly, her room was stifling. She couldn't bear it any longer. She tore herself from the window and strode into the hall, the floorboards mercifully cool beneath her bare feet. She began to descend the stairs, her hand sliding down the smooth banister, judging her progress in the dark by its familiar bumps and whorls.

And stopped halfway down, arrested by the sight of Silas standing in the foyer below, as pale and unearthly as a specter. He wasn't wearing his servant's uniform, but rather the suit she had once seen him wearing in the city streets, his hair tied back with a matching black ribbon. He had removed his gloves; one of them peeked from his pocket, a neatly folded square of pearl-gray kidskin.

He had been outside the house. She wasn't certain how she knew—only that it would be very like Silas to be able to get past the wards without telling them, and there seemed to be a faint smell of winter in the foyer, as though a trickle of cold, clean air had wafted inside at his heels.

He didn't turn. It took her a moment to realize that he was so deep in thought he hadn't noticed her. The idea came as a shock—wrong somehow, unsettling. In all the time she'd known him, she had never caught him unawares. Then she noticed what he was looking at: the empty space on the wall beside the portraits of Alistair, Charlotte, and Maximilian. The space where Nathaniel's portrait would hang one day after he died.

And perhaps her own portrait too.

Slowly, she trailed down the remaining steps. Silas noticed her then. He didn't move, but he stiffened slightly before she reached out and took his icy hand. While he didn't clasp hers in return, neither did he pull away.

"What was she like?" she asked quietly, studying Charlotte's portrait. Once again it struck her that though Nathaniel had inherited his father's looks, he shared the laughter in his mother's eyes.

"Singular. A woman of integrity." Admiration shaded his dry, whispering voice, as faint as old cobwebs stirring in a breeze. "From time to time she bade me watch over her children while she and Alistair were away."

"She trusted you."

"In a sense. She trusted I would not have welcomed the histrionics occasioned by the death or injury of my master's infant sons."

Doubtless there was far more to it than that, but she said nothing, knowing how carefully Silas guarded his privacy. One poorly chosen word, and this fragile moment between them might shatter.

"She would have liked you," he said at last. "Very much, I believe."

Pain lodged in her chest like an arrow. Gazing at his elegant face in profile, etched by the foyer's dimmed lamps, she thought of the ostrich room—the dusty opera ticket he had tucked into his jacket. And she recalled the peace on his face when he had walked into the Archon's circle, embracing his own destruction. There was a mercy afforded mortals that Silas would never receive. He would never be the one to die first.

Her throat aching, she brought his hand to her lips and kissed it. His pale skin was as cold and flawless as alabaster. She could feel his claws, and even those were dear to her.

"Mistress?" His voice betrayed nothing, but she

suspected that for once, she had surprised him.

"I want you to know—when we die, we won't leave you alone. We'll make sure of it. I promise."

He turned to look at her. Something terrible shone in his eyes: a brutal and pitiless inhuman grief, a grief that could devour worlds. For an instant, fear sank its talons into Elisabeth's heart. Then he smiled, and the moment passed, leaving his face as beautiful and calm as new-fallen snow.

"Come," he said. "There is something I wish to show you."

He drew her out of the foyer and into the dining room, toward a section of blank wall between two glass-doored cabinets. "What—" she began, but stopped when he touched the wallpaper, which melted away to nothing, revealing a doorway that hadn't been there before.

They stepped into an empty ballroom, its tall arched windows glittering with moonlight, casting fractured pools across the marble floor. Elisabeth's gasp echoed, scattering against the high ceiling like a flock of birds taking flight.

Mirrors along the walls multiplied their reflections

into infinity, creating the illusion of a vast space popu-
lated with hundreds of their own doubles, endless
replicas of Elisabeth gazing around openmouthed. A
balcony soared above them, its railings winking dimly
beneath a patina of dust, dizzying against the half-seen
frescoes that decorated the ceiling in delicate shades of
blue and gold. Three lowered chandeliers rested on the
floor, tilted at angles, as though they had grown sleepy
and collapsed there like fairy-tale maidens in great
tiered gowns of crystal and candle wax.

Every step they took rippled across the mirrors.
Elisabeth found herself transfixed for a moment by
their reflections: Silas slight and formal in his reserved
black evening dress; herself clad in a nightgown, holding his hand.

His soft voice wove through the spell. "The last
time the ballroom was opened, it was for the Midwinter Ball of 1807, and Master Thorn was an infant.
He has no memory of this place. Forgive me, mistress,
for not looking after it properly. You must imagine it
as it was eighteen years ago—the chandeliers raised,
the candles lit, the frescoes enchanted to move. A string
quartet played in the corner, and an ice sculpture stood

at the center of the room, turning the breath of those who stood near it to frost." He released her hand and stepped back, lifting an arm toward the doorway. "The guests entered in pairs, dressed in their finest coats and gowns."

Her breath caught. As though a layer of dust had blown away from every surface, she saw the candlelight glittering on the balconies. She heard the music, saw the painted clouds drift across the ceiling. She imagined the dancers swirling past, cast into eternity by the mirrors.

The enchantment of it tugged at her heart. She had never danced before. She didn't know how, or if she could learn.

It wasn't that she was clumsy; it was just that she existed in a world that wasn't designed for women her size. It was easy to bang into doorframes designed for people half a head shorter, or knock over chairs trying to fold her long legs out from under a cramped table. She knew this, and yet . . .

The vision of ghostly dancers hovering before her eyes, the strains of phantom music trembling in her ears, she steeled herself and turned to Silas. "Will you teach me how to dance?"

He smiled. It was clear that he had been expecting her to ask. In fact, that was the reason why he had brought her here.

"You taught Nathaniel, too, didn't you," she said as understanding dawned.

"Once upon a time, though not without considerable persuasion. He has squandered my efforts ever since."

She remembered the gossip at Ashcroft's manor— that Nathaniel never danced at parties. "He'll dance with me."

"That is my hope, mistress. Shall we begin?"

Anxiety scampered through her, and she stomped it down like an errant booklouse. Dancing couldn't be harder than slaying fiends. "What do I need to do?"

"Here. Like so." He took her right hand in his left, placing the other lightly at her waist. "It would be better if you were to lead, given your height, but it won't matter here, I think. Master Thorn is nearly as tall as you; he will be able to see his surroundings well enough . . ."

Then he began to move, guiding her in slow, graceful circles. She spent the first few rotations frowning in fierce concentration at her feet, until his hand vanished from her waist to lift her chin with a single clawed finger. She immediately stepped on his boot.

"Better myself than Master Thorn," he said, his eyes aglow with amusement. "Worry not, mistress. I am unhurt. And you will never learn if you watch your feet so."

He was right. Soon the steps began to come more naturally to her, the dance's rhythm almost instinctual, as though the knowledge had always lain dormant within her. Around them, their doubles flowed across the surfaces of the mirrors. She pictured how it would look during a ball: colorful gowns eddying like flowers caught in a river's current, infinitely turning, the women's jewels sparkling in the candlelight. Her footprints in the dust on the marble floor formed neater and neater circles, as though left across a fine powder of snow.

It seemed impossible that dancing could be so easy. This exhilarating lack of effort, she was sure, owed itself entirely to Silas's expertise. Though he never seemed to be controlling her movements, she occasionally felt him adjust her stance with a subtle lift of her arm or slight pressure of his hand against her waist, accompanied by a murmured instruction. All the while his gaze flicked over her, evaluating her posture and the positioning of her feet. "Very good," he said at last.

Where had he learned this? Were demons taught to dance, or was it another skill, like cooking, that he had acquired in the human realm? She imagined him going out at night, moving unseen within society, studying dancers and fashions, a spare, pale observer unnoticed in his dark suit and attention-diverting glamour. Always alone, his youthful face unchanging as the centuries passed.

With a sting of mortification, she realized how childish her promise had been. It was all well and good to vow not to leave him alone after she and Nathaniel died, but what about a hundred years from now? Two hundred? When the pair of them existed only in Silas's memories, their bones long dust—what then? With a swift, almost shocking intensity, her throat tightened and her eyes stung.

"Mistress," Silas admonished. He produced a handkerchief and steered her toward a bench along the wall. The moment they sat, she pulled him into a tight embrace. He went very still, his muscles rigid. Then, after a delicate pause, he sighed and placed a hand on her back.

"I'm sorry," she said, her face buried against his shoulder.

"It is well."

It wasn't. She loved him. She loved him as much she did Nathaniel, with an intensity almost too powerful to bear.

What did it mean to love a demon? Not merely to care for him, pity him—but to love him?

"You are tired," Silas remarked after some time. Rising, he gathered her into his arms as though she weighed nothing. Her size didn't matter; she felt the iron strength in his slender body as he carried her out of the ballroom and toward the stairs.

She hadn't realized until then how weary she was and how cold, her feet numb from the cold marble floor. Wondering distantly if he had glamoured her to escape from her embrace, she let her eyes drift shut. The world floated past. For a moment it seemed she might stay there forever, weightlessly suspended in his arms—but then she felt the softness of her bed beneath her, sinking under her weight as he set her down, and the covers being drawn up to her chin.

She wrested her eyes open, watching through heavy

lashes as Silas finished smoothing the blanket and paused to touch her hair. She knew without looking that his claws had brushed the silver strands.

"Will you stay until I fall asleep?" she whispered when he drew away.

He stopped halfway toward the door, considering, his face expressionless in the dark. "Yes," he said finally. "If you wish."

SEVEN

THE NEXT MORNING, Elisabeth woke to a rap on her door. She sat up in a rustle of bedsheets, filled with sleepy contentment until she remembered her challenge to Nathaniel the day before. Instantly, she went from groggy to wide awake.

She grabbed Demonslayer from the nightstand and pulled the covers around herself like a thick cape, swaddling everything but her face. Thus defended, she croaked, "Come in."

The door cracked open a few inches, accompanied by a jangling of crockery and a muffled swear. Then Nathaniel wedged himself into view, holding the door open with the side of a breakfast tray.

She watched in trepidation. The last time he had

tried cooking breakfast, he had nearly banished the kitchen into a void dimension. The primordial sludge that Silas had scraped from the frying pan, emitting a faint scream on its way to the waste bucket, had given her nightmares for weeks. Mistrustfully, she eyed the tray's silver dome, reminded of Mercy's overturned dustbin, which was still rattling its way aggressively around the first floor.

"Nothing beneath there is alive," Nathaniel assured her cheerfully, squeezing the rest of the way inside. "At least not the last time I checked." He set the tray on the foot of her bed, retreating—in a rather cowardly fashion, she thought—to the stool in front of her vanity, conveniently located beside the door. "Enjoy your breakfast, my dearest darling. I cooked all of it myself, with barely any assistance from sorcery whatsoever."

Elisabeth shuddered. Holding Demonslayer at the ready in one hand, she cautiously lifted the dome with the other.

And stared. Before her eyes lay piles of toast with blackberry preserves, arranged beside greasy spiced sausages still crackling from the pan. A bowl of strawberries glistened red beneath a snowy heap of thickly whipped cream. The scrambled eggs were as fluffy as clouds, garnished with a scattering of green chives and a sprig of parsley.

Mouth watering at the smell, she looked at Nathaniel in disbelief. "*You* made this? Not Silas?"

"He gave me instructions, but I suspect that only made it harder. For someone who's never tasted human food, he has very strong opinions about the correct way to dice chives."

Gingerly, she lifted one of the slices of toast to peer beneath it. When a further inspection unearthed nothing suspicious, she cautiously took a bite of the eggs, braced herself, and chewed. Her eyes widened in amazement.

Before she could find words, the manor responded for her: the curtains whisked open, flooding the room with light, sparkling on the tray's crystal vase, which she noticed for the first time held a single red rose.

She had sampled a bite of sausage and devoured half a piece of toast before she paused to check on Nathaniel, who was sitting with his chin propped on his hands and a fond look in his eyes. Had he been watching her eat? She hesitated, taking in his unusual pallor.

He looked as though he had been up all night.

Suddenly feeling tentative, she leaned forward for a better view out the window. The cyclone hadn't gone away, but the debris was visibly thinner than before, speared with bright shafts of sunlight. "I think it's working," she said.

A shadow crossed Nathaniel's face, there and gone again so quickly that Elisabeth felt sure she must have imagined it. "Or breakfast in bed is on Aunt Clothilde's list of approved activities for well-behaved suitors. I hope she doesn't expect me to do it again, because I'm not sure I'll ever be allowed back in the kitchen. Don't go downstairs for a while, by the way."

Before Elisabeth could process this cryptic advice, Mercy poked her head inside, wearing a guarded expression. "Did anyone know there's a ballroom next to the dining room?"

"So that's where it got off to. By now I was wondering if it had packed up and left for another sorcerer's house. That happens occasionally," he explained. "Ballrooms are extremely high-maintenance."

Mercy looked doubtful. Elisabeth, for her part, was simply grateful for the proof that she hadn't hallucinated last night's events. The memory of Silas teaching her to dance felt fragile, unreal, as though spun from moonlight and gossamer. She had last seen him sitting in the chair beside her bed as she fell asleep, but the cushion bore no impression of his weight.

"What's that in your hair?" she asked Mercy, noticing the dark, sticky substance matting the strands escaping from the other girl's bun.

"You don't want to know," Mercy said grimly, and left.

She found out after breakfast, when she ignored Nathaniel's increasingly creative attempts to lure her into the upstairs solar. The entire first floor of the manor had been swamped by a sticky dark purple tide, which had splashed up on the baseboards and stairs like wet tar, filling the air with a distinctive sweet fragrance. She bent to stick her finger in the substance, then tasted it. Just as she had thought: blackberry preserves.

"Barely any assistance from sorcery whatsoever," she remarked.

"To be fair, we'd run out, and it wasn't as though I could go to the market for another jar. Don't worry, the spell will wear off in a few hours."

Elisabeth wasn't worried. She dipped her finger back in and ate some more.

She spent the remainder of the morning deep in thought, pacing the manor's halls with her knuckles pressed to her mouth and her loose hair hanging in a curtain around her face. Nathaniel had requested another impossible task by lunch.

Hoping that a change of scenery might inspire her, she climbed one of the tiny hidden stairs that led to the servants' quarters. When she stepped out at the top, stooping so she didn't bump her head, she found herself in a place entirely unlike the rest of the manor. Sunlight poured through rusty-framed windows set into the angled ceiling, illuminating worn floorboards and flaking whitewashed plaster, the presence of a stool, a bucket, and a few abandoned rags the only sign of past habitation. Shadows flickered across the walls as though cast by a passing flock of birds. Peering outside, she felt even more certain than before that the whirlwind surrounding the house had diminished; many of the largest chunks of masonry seemed to have reattached themselves to the roof.

Her exploration of the floor uncovered a number of small, abandoned rooms, their bed frames bare and their old mattresses leaned against the walls. In one she discovered a nest of stolen treasures heaped in the far corner—dusty costume jewelry, a silver fork, and an old sock that she recognized as one of Nathaniel's, missing since last November. Most likely, they had been hoarded by Volume XI during its time living up here as a feral.

She was turning to go back downstairs when she caught sight of a room that appeared to be still in use. Through its cracked door she glimpsed an armoire and a narrow, neatly made bed. Curious, she stepped forward, brushing the door open wider with her fingertips.

Her heart gave a peculiar twist. She had wondered before whether Silas had a room in the manor—a place where he kept his clothes, if not to sleep. Now she had her answer. Her eyes roamed across the porcelain washbasin on the nightstand and the items laid out on the armoire, arranged with careful precision: a pair of gloves, a folded handkerchief, one of the ribbons he used to tie his hair. It felt almost wrong to see these mundane objects separated from Silas, evidence that despite his immortality, he rose and washed and dressed himself like anyone else. Even having seen him almost naked in the summoning circle, it was somehow surreal to imagine that he ever took off his uniform.

And then there were the drawings. An easel stood by the window, laden with sheets of paper, sticks of charcoal lined up along the ledge beneath. More papers leaned against the wall and lay stacked in piles. There was something indefinably old-fashioned about the scene, as though borrowed from the studio of a seventeenth-century artist.

She stood mesmerized, taking in the black-and-white sketches of Brassbridge's cathedrals and parks, of people sitting alone, holding hands, drinking tea, all of them composed of more than light and shadow—somehow, Silas had recorded their souls. They were beautiful, and deeply lonely, though she couldn't say exactly why. Perhaps because many of the subjects were centuries gone, not just the people but the city itself: she recognized familiar streets altered by time, buildings she knew standing beside others long demolished. The faces, too, she was sure, had belonged to real people— people that perhaps he had known . . .

Her eyes caught on a charcoal portrait of Nathaniel. Silas had captured him grinning, looking to one side, a lock of hair falling across his forehead. A hint of some darker, sadder emotion hardened the edges of his laughing eyes, giving him the look of someone struggling to smile through the pain of a wound. It was so true to life that her breath stopped. Other likenesses peeked out from behind the innumerable cityscapes, rendering Nathaniel at different ages and in various attitudes: trying on a coat, deep in concentration at his desk, caught in a rare moment of peaceful slumber.

But the half-finished portrait on the easel wasn't of him. It was of her. Before she could stop herself, she took a step inside.

It wasn't like looking in a mirror—it was something more. Silas had drawn her with a smudge of ink standing out on her unsmiling features, her tangled hair wreathing her face. Her eyes shone fiercely with hope and courage and resolve, the gaze of an avenging saint, radiant with purpose. To the viewer, her expression seemed to promise either salvation or judgment. Perhaps, for some, both at once.

Elisabeth stood frozen, arrested by the image.

Is that what I look like? Is that how he sees me?

She half expected Silas's whispering voice to answer, but when she looked over her shoulder, the hallway was empty.

She shivered. The desire to venture deeper into the room, to see his other drawings and the secrets they might hold, burned within her like thirst. At last she tore herself away, carefully moving the door back to its original position. If Silas had wanted her to see this, he would have shown it to her. Perhaps, one day, he would.

She felt strangely adrift climbing back down the staircase, but the portrait had given her an idea. She paid another visit to the attic. Then she went to the muniment room and sorted through its older drawers, reading through lists upon lists of carpets purchased, antiques sold, and portraits commissioned, surrounded by the peaceable rustling of contented grimoires. Finally, she found what she was looking for.

Placed in storage, the curse deemed unbreakable . . .

She delivered the task over lunch. Afterward, Nathaniel's behavior grew highly enigmatic. Once the blackberry preserves had vanished (Mercy confided to Elisabeth that Silas had spent the whole morning in cat form, refusing to leave his perch atop the kitchen cupboard), he made Elisabeth stay in his study while he prepared. To pass the time, she retrieved a grimoire from the shelves. When she had first seen it late last autumn, it had been particularly sad and neglected, the gilt on its cover flaking off with melancholy. Now it had been restored to a cheery robin's-egg blue, gold designs of roses, songbirds, and leaping hares surrounding its title: Austermeer's Complete Fairy Tales. All this time, she had never had the chance to read it.

When she opened it, she discovered a handwritten dedication on the patterned endpapers: *To my beloved— may you always believe in fairy tales*. Smiling, she traced her fingers over the letters, feeling the indentations they had left on the paper. This was one of the things she loved best about books. She might never know who had written the dedication, or how long ago, or to whom, but she could briefly clasp hands with them across eternity, a chance meeting of souls made possible by their shared love of a story.

A second surprise awaited her a moment later: the grimoire's blue ribbon already marked a familiar chapter heading, *The Three Impossible Tasks*.

"Did you do that on purpose?" she asked. Perhaps it had been listening to her conversation with Nathaniel the day before. But it replied by fluttering its ribbon at her in emphatic denial. It ruffled its pages, flipping to another chapter entitled *The Orphan Prince*, and then back to *The Three Impossible Tasks*. It was trying to communicate something, but she wasn't certain what. Puzzled, she settled down to read.

The illustrations moved in this grimoire too, but they were more detailed, lavishly depicting the moonlit tower in which the princess lay sleeping, its stones overgrown with rose vines. After she had finished the story, lingering on the page in which the peasant boy held aloft a jar of reflected starlight, she turned back to *The Orphan Prince*. Reading it left her no more enlightened than before. It was a simple tale about a prince who was lost in the wilderness as a baby, only to be raised first by a hare, then an owl, a fox, and a wolf, learning important lessons from each one. She was studying the illustration of his coronation as king when a bang echoed from overhead.

Curiosity overcame her. Creeping over to the study's door and straining her ears, she detected more sounds: distant thumps and bangs, the creaking of the stairs; once a loud clatter, followed by a strong smell of aetherial combustion. What these might indicate, she couldn't guess.

Nathaniel joined them late for dinner, his hair more disheveled than she had ever seen it, with his sleeves singed and a scorch mark across one cheek. He bolted down his food as though he were at risk of starving to death and then vanished again into the manor's depths, hardly uttering a word.

"Never fear, mistress," Silas said that night, closing her bedroom's curtains against the dark. "Master Thorn is equal to the task. Were he not, I would be with him now, airing my opinion on the matter."

This, Elisabeth could believe. "So he isn't in any danger?"

Silas merely smiled. "Good night, mistress," he said softly, slipping out the door.

She awoke the next morning to a peculiar series of sounds. A clank. A scrape. A metallic squeal. These noises were accompanied by a whispered conversation, snatches of which she caught through the door, saying things like "Quiet!" and "You'll wake her!" Finally, Elisabeth couldn't stand it any longer. She leaped out of bed and flung open the door.

She was vaguely aware of Mercy dodging around a corner, leaving Nathaniel in the hallway by himself. But her attention was fixed on the vision in front of her.

He had brought her the suit of armor from the attic, gleaming on its stand as though newly forged.

"It's de-cursed," Nathaniel announced, slightly out of breath. "And Silas advised me on a few adjustments to the fit, but it was already nearly the right size."

"Can I touch it?"

"Go ahead. It's for you."

Elisabeth stepped forward. Wonderingly, her fingers grazed the cold, polished metal, catching a little on the thorn engravings and bumping over the seams. She could hardly breathe. She had only felt this way twice in her life: first when she had received her Collegium greatkey at age thirteen, and second upon finding out that Director Irena had left her Demonslayer in her will.

At the very edge of her perception, she was aware of Nathaniel watching her, not smiling, but instead studying her expression as though he were memorizing it to be tucked away for future perusal, like a letter that would one day grow worn and creased with care.

"It isn't as though you need it," he said, his voice deceptively light. "You're already terrifyingly indestructible. But I'm glad you like it."

"I do," she answered thickly. "Nathaniel, I love it. Thank you."

"The front door's opening again!" Mercy yelled from downstairs.

She forced her eyes from the armor. "How did you do it? The curse was supposed to be unbreakable."

Leaning against the wall, he grinned. "Let's just say that sorcery has made considerable advances since the 1600s."

"I think—I'd like to try it on."

A brief setback ensued when it turned out he hadn't thought that far ahead—the windows darkened in response, and the shutters started rattling ominously— but Silas swiftly came to their rescue carrying a folded bundle of Nathaniel's clothes, which were more practical to wear beneath a suit of armor than a nightgown. Then she stoically held still as Silas instructed him in the method of putting on each piece ("It is a great deal of iron, mistress, so I would prefer not to touch it, even with gloves"), tortured by the sensation of his long fingers deftly buckling on greaves and pauldrons, his warmth close and his breath feather-soft on her skin.

When at last he finished, his pupils were dark. It seemed to require some effort for him to draw away and tip down the helmet's visor.

"The topiaries are still prowling around out there," he offered, his voice echoing tinnily in her ears. "Do you think you might be up for a rematch?"

A few hours and dozens of decapitated topiaries later, Elisabeth felt unstoppable. She'd had to take a break eventually, but with the armor on, she was very nearly a match for Thorn Manor's wards. At the end, several of the topiaries hadn't been able to grow their heads back, and had slunk off around the corner in disgrace.

She wore the armor for the rest of the day. She clanked happily through the halls. She clanked cheerfully up and down the stairs. Relieving herself proved something of an inconvenience, but this, too, she mastered after some strategic unbuckling in the powder room. When night fell, she was tempted to see what sleeping in the armor would feel like, until Silas gave her a disapproving look and she submitted to its removal immediately.

Nathaniel seemed oddly relieved. He had spent the afternoon pretending to have various critical chores to do, which consisted mainly of striding around the manor looking harassed, then pausing to stare at her when he thought she wasn't looking. It was obvious he was pretending, because he never did chores; and anyway, she couldn't think of any that would require him to pace back and forth between the dining room and the foyer, vigorously unbuttoning his collar.

She had an unsettling dream that night. She was a knight standing beside a throne in a great flickering hall, unable to move. She wanted to tell Nathaniel that the armor hadn't been de-cursed after all, and had trapped her inside, but when she tried to open her mouth, she couldn't make a sound. He was the king in this dream, but his throne sat empty; he knelt instead at the foot of the dais, where a summoning circle was carved into the stone. As she watched, he spilled his blood across it, whispering a name Elisabeth couldn't hear. A frantic terror seized her. Which name had he used? Silas, or Silariathas?

When Silas appeared above him, it was impossible to tell—he looked as he always did in the summoning circle, gaunt and black-eyed with hunger. Except this time he held a crown aloft over Nathaniel's bowed head. Elisabeth tried and failed to shout a warning. She knew something terrible would happen when the crown descended.

A scream pierced the awful tableau. She jerked awake, her muscles tingling with dread. For a moment she couldn't move, just like in the dream, listening paralyzed as the scream cut off with a ragged sob. Then her head cleared, and she exploded into action. Throwing back the covers, she grabbed Demonslayer and pocketed a handful of salt rounds from the nightstand's drawer.

Out in the hallway, the manor looked subtly different: a console table was missing, and a painting hung on a normally blank wall. This, Silas had explained to her, was how the manor had looked during Nathaniel's childhood. It wasn't real, but rather an illusion like the one he had created for the Royal Ball, conjured by his dreaming mind. If Elisabeth walked over to where she knew the table was, she would stub her toe on it even though she couldn't see it.

She was tempted to try, just to be sure. The unearthly screaming had ended, and a faint smell of soil and rot filled the air. This wasn't the nightmare in which blood seeped from the walls, or Alistair Thorn's specter went staggering down the hallway, clutching his slit throat; it wasn't even the new one where Silas's hoarse, tortured voice whispered from drains and closets, pleading for their help.

She almost wished it were.

Rounding the corner, she nearly collided with Mercy's stiff back. The girl stood petrified, staring into the darkness beyond the dimmed lamps. Elisabeth could just make out a woman's figure, standing oddly slumped to one side and wearing a long dirt-crusted shroud. Elisabeth's stomach plunged. She knew from experience that she didn't want to look at the woman's face too closely. Before the features could resolve into focus, she threw one of her salt rounds, and the illusion vanished in a puff of sparkling white.

Mercy jumped when Elisabeth touched her shoulder. "It's just another nightmare," she said.

"This is a bad one," Mercy noted, pale.

"If you want to—" She broke off, remembering

Mercy's bravery with the broom and mop. If Elisabeth told her she could hide in the kitchen, she wouldn't go; she would feel like she was running away. "You could make us a pot of tea," she suggested instead, inspiration striking. "Nathaniel might like some when he wakes up."

Mercy jerked her head in a nod and gratefully made for the stairs, glancing over her shoulder as she went.

The nightmares usually didn't affect the kitchen—Elisabeth thought perhaps because Nathaniel didn't have any bad memories associated with it. The thought made her chest squeeze with sorrow, even as her heart pounded deafeningly in her ears. She started down the hallway again, breaking into a run. As she neared Nathaniel's bedroom, the woman reappeared, standing just beyond the light. This time Elisabeth ran past her without interfering, resisting the terrible urge to turn and look. That face bore no resemblance to the portrait hanging in the foyer, Charlotte with her gentle smile and sparkling eyes.

Nathaniel's door stood open. Inside, she found him still in bed, rammed against the headboard, his face bloodless and his nightshirt unlaced down the front, the scars from his duel with Ashcroft standing out in stark relief. He was shaking so badly she could see the strands of his hair trembling. A glass lay on the floor at his bedside, a stain soaking the carpet beneath it—his medicine.

He must have knocked it from Silas's hand. The demon sat at his side, but Nathaniel barely seemed aware of his presence, even when Silas gripped his face and forcibly turned his head. His eyes remained trained on the corner of the room.

"Master, there is nothing there."

"You're wrong," Nathaniel answered hoarsely. "I can see it."

"I would not allow such a thing in the house."

"How can you say that? You helped him—you carried—" His voice broke. "You carried the bodies for him. I *saw* you."

Silas briefly closed his eyes. Then he looked to Elisabeth, his gaze luminous with an unspoken request.

Haltingly, she entered, and at last saw what Nathaniel's eyes were fixed upon: a thing that had once been a child standing in the corner of the room, covered in grave dirt. Horror washed over her. She had witnessed many terrible things during Nathaniel's nightmares, but she had never seen his younger brother, Maximilian.

Just an illusion, she reminded herself, reaching for her salt rounds. A moment later, all that remained of the awful specter was a glittering white cloud.

Nathaniel looked at her in astonishment, as though she were the one who had worked magic, not him. She set Demonslayer down and clambered straight onto the bed. A moment later she was gathering him into her arms, holding him tightly.

Silas stood, went to the window, and looked out.

"I was dreaming," Nathaniel said roughly, only now coming to the realization. Elisabeth didn't answer, just stroked his sweaty hair.

"Give me the third task," he mumbled, his voice muffled against her chest.

"Right now?"

"Yes."

He wanted something else to think about, she realized. She had to swallow before she could speak. "Take me ice-skating. You promised."

Painfully, he laughed. Her throat tightened with—what? Surely it was inappropriate to want to kiss him at a time like this. And yet the longing overpowered her. She wanted to kiss his exposed shoulder, his scarred collarbone, the nape of his neck, as though in doing so she could drive away his demons.

All of them but one, who still stood gazing out the window. "Master," he said softly. "Mistress." He drew the curtain open wider, letting in a breath of cold.

Elisabeth sat up to look. Her eyes widened. Normally the window showed a charming view of jumbled, slanting rooftops, with the Great Library and Magisterium's towers rising in the distance. Lower down it offered a glimpse of the manor's small garden, with its draggled plants and thorn hedge hemmed in by a wrought iron fence.

Or at least, it had used to.

Now a vista more befitting the grounds of an estate lay beyond the panes. Only a tantalizing glimpse of it showed between the curtains: the geometric patterns of a hedge maze, its moonlit shadows inscribed on the snow. At first she had the wild thought that the manor had changed locations, transported itself straight out of the city. Then she saw the distant lights of Brassbridge glittering beyond the maze—still there, winking like an altar of windblown candles as the cyclone's debris hurtled past.

She glanced reflexively at Nathaniel, and found him wearing an expression of strained recognition. "I haven't seen the formal gardens since my mother died," he said, his voice still hoarse from screaming. "They vanished that same night, and never returned."

Silas inclined his head. "It has been a long while since there was last a lady of the house."

Elisabeth shivered. On impulse, she placed a hand on the wall above Nathaniel's bed. There was something there—not so different from the feeling when she touched a grimoire and felt the consciousness stirring beneath its cover, the magic coursing through it like a living pulse.

"I think the manor wants us to go outside."

EIGHT

SILAS HAD ALREADY selected a pair of dressing gowns from the chest of drawers. He helped Elisabeth into the first, and handed Nathaniel's cane to him as he drew the second over his master's shoulders. They were lacing on their boots when Mercy appeared at the door with tea.

Elisabeth's heart fell. They couldn't leave her alone after the horror of Nathaniel's nightmare. She opened her mouth to say they would meet her in the parlor, delaying their trip outside, but Silas smoothly intervened.

"Thank you, Mercy. Master Thorn and Mistress Scrivener will be leaving us, but I find myself in need of company. If you would be kind enough to bring the tray to the drawing room, I will join you momentarily."

Knowing that even Mercy's most painstaking effort at tea wasn't likely to meet Silas's impossible standards, regardless of the fact that he couldn't taste it, Elisabeth placed a grateful hand on his arm.

He didn't acknowledge the touch, his gaze fixed on the now-empty hall. "I trust I shall endure," he murmured, almost inaudibly, as though striving to convince himself.

They proceeded downstairs through the ballroom, where a grand pair of glass double doors—they had been windows last night, she was certain—let out onto a sweeping stone terrace. Here they waited while Silas brought them their coats. Once Elisabeth had been tucked into her warm fur-lined pelisse, she went to press her nose to the glass. She recognized the fountain, though it was now three times its previous size, the sculpture of a lone mermaid joined by carvings of nymphs and rearing horses locked in tumbling cascades of ice. She wondered how this all looked from the street—whether the yard appeared the same to passersby, or whether it had expanded suddenly in size, shunting the neighboring houses to either side.

She was mulling this over when she saw Nathaniel's reflection in the window pause and turn toward Silas, his expression grave. He looked remarkably collected now, unaffected by his nightmare save for a lingering pallor, tall and imposing in his dark wool greatcoat.

Sensing a private moment, she quickly resumed studying the garden, but his words nevertheless carried across the echoing ballroom: "I'm sorry for what I said earlier."

"You spoke only the truth," Silas replied, his whispering voice barely audible.

"Still. You were acting under my father's orders."

Silas gave Nathaniel an indecipherable look. Then he reached for his coat collar, neatly turning it up against the cold. "There is little I will not do in service to House Thorn. It is fortunate for this world that you are a better man than your father."

Briefly, the chill radiating from the glass stole Elisabeth's breath. Double vision overcame her: instead of fussing with Nathaniel's coat, Silas was standing over him holding a crown. Then she blinked, and the image vanished. Nathaniel was beside her, turning the latch on the door.

A storm of snowflakes whirled past them, sucked inside by the warmth. The frozen air snapped at her nose and cheeks, and her first breath stung with cold. When the door shut behind them, she reached for Nathaniel's hand. His gloved fingers closed around her mitten.

A wintry hush swallowed the city's usual nocturnal sounds. After the muted clattering of a night cab's wheels receded into the distance, the stillness was profound. They paused for a moment in mutual silence, taking in the view from the terrace. She felt almost as though she had wandered into one of Silas's charcoal drawings, a secretive world of white snow and black branches, luminous in the night. She wondered what Nathaniel was seeing beside her—if he was remembering what the gardens looked like in full bloom, vibrant with life and color. Then they started for the steps that led down to the maze, snow crunching beneath their boots. Dark hedges beckoned, interspersed with marble statues overgrown with vines.

"How does all of this fit?" she asked, her breath puffing white in the dark. "Is it a separate dimension, like Prendergast's workshop?"

"No, which is why it's illegal." He grinned at her from behind his upturned collar. "Magicking away a few bedchambers is one thing, but I'm told the sorcery used to maintain the garden warps reality in nearby areas of the city."

"And they've let you keep it?"

"It's like the wards. Pre-Reforms spells are grand-fathered in for old houses."

"That seems rather corrupt," Elisabeth observed.

Amusement sparkled in Nathaniel's eyes. "We can go back inside if you like."

"No!" she blurted out, gripping his hand a little tighter. Embarrassed, she tried to put on a stern expression. "The damage is already done. I suppose the Collegium knows about it?"

"Naturally. Director Marius used to look like he was sucking a lemon every time someone mentioned the backward clocks on Staircross Avenue."

"Then we might as well enjoy it, since it's already here."

"I must admit, I'm shocked." He raised his eyebrows. "Am I corrupting you, Elisabeth Scrivener?"

She was about to jab him in the side when he gestured for silence. Catching her eye, he released her hand to point. A giraffe topiary was watching them from a bend ahead. Seeing them looking, it came to life and slunk off, vanishing deeper into the maze. A moment later a handful of other leafy heads rose into view in the distance; then they, too, confirming the news of Elisabeth's arrival, hastily made themselves scarce.

"So this is where they live," she said, suppressing a twinge of guilt. They had attacked first, she reminded herself.

Nathaniel regarded her in fascination. "Where did you think they came from?"

"When you've grown up in a library with talking books for friends, there are some things you don't think to question."

His laugh cut through the air, then faded. They had turned a corner, coming upon a snow-covered bench beneath a leafless arbor. A single white rose rested atop it, its petals glistening with frost. Nathaniel trailed to a stop.

"This was my mother's favorite spot in the garden. I had nearly forgotten." He stepped closer, lifting the rose from the snow.

Elisabeth supposed someone might have left it there before the garden vanished, leaving it magically preserved for years, but that didn't seem likely. She remembered Silas standing in the foyer surrounded by the smell of winter air, and thought there was a far simpler explanation.

"I would have liked to have known her," she said softly.

"The two of you would have gotten along. She used to read to Max and me from a book of fairy tales. A grimoire—Father gave it to her on the eve of their wedding." An unhappy smile twisted his mouth. "Because their love was like a fairy tale, he said."

Austermeer's Complete Fairy Tales, she thought, a chill passing through her. The dedication had been written by Alistair to Charlotte. No wonder the grimoire had been consumed by such a sense of melancholy.

"What happened?" she asked. "All Silas told me was that they died in an accident."

He shook his head, but not in disagreement. "They went to watch a boat race on the river. The pier was old—there were too many spectators. It collapsed under their weight. Nearly a dozen people drowned."

He turned the rose in his gloved fingers, his expression distant. "The story was all over the papers for weeks. There were dozens of theories—that it was sabotage, an assassination. No one could believe that a magister's wife and son had died in a mere accident."

"The reporters," she said, her heart catching on a painful beat. "I never realized." He had always made his aversion to the press seem like a joke.

"They tried to corner me at the funeral. I was supposed to have been with Mother and Max at the pier that day, but I wasn't feeling well, so I stayed home in bed at the last minute. I remember one headline—'Thorn Legacy Saved by a Runny Nose.'"

Her hand had clenched into a fist. "That's awful. Where was—" She caught herself. "Where was your father?" She had been about to say "Silas" instead.

"Away on magister's business, which made things even worse. I came downstairs when I heard screaming, but the housekeeper wouldn't tell me the news—no one would tell me what had happened until Father got back. And then he was so grief-stricken he couldn't bring himself to speak to me. In the end, Silas was the one who sat me down and explained everything."

Elisabeth could easily picture this scene, a young, shocked, pale Nathaniel sitting across from Silas in the drawing room, an epicenter of unearthly calm in a house overturned with chaos . . .

She closed the distance between them to fold him into an embrace, clumsy in her coat and mittens. Nathaniel's arm came around her, holding her close. They remained that way for a long moment. Then he carefully set the rose back down in the same position he had found it in. His eyes met hers over the edge of his collar, their gray depths bruised.

"That was the day I learned that fairy tales are a lie."

Elisabeth's heart strained. A cloud of mingled breath hung in the air between them, warm and slightly damp against her lips. "Not every story has a happy ending," she offered. "But most do, if you're brave enough to keep reading to the end."

"How can you be so certain?" He searched her face as though she were a strange, rare marvel—a flower blooming from cobblestones, or an unexpected light in the distant dark.

"I've read a lot of them," she said seriously.

Brokenly, he laughed.

She took his hand. "Have you ever seen what's at the center of the maze?"

"A few times." He was clearly relieved to change the subject. "It isn't much—just an ornamental pool with some fish. Max and I always suspected they ate each other to survive."

"We might as well go look," she said, tugging him onward.

"That isn't a bad idea." His voice lightened. "Did you bring Demonslayer? By now, the cannibalism may have escalated."

She shook her head, smiling, but on the inside she thrummed with a strange mixture of uncertainty and anticipation. Ever since touching the wall above Nathaniel's bed, she had the sense that the manor was leading them somewhere—that it wanted to show them something.

They passed the final turn in the hedge, reaching an overgrown archway guarded by a pair of statues. Beyond lay a frozen pond, its bank curving against a frost-white willow tree and a stone gazebo, much larger than what she had imagined based on Nathaniel's description. He drew up short. She could tell by his expression that this wasn't what he had expected to find either.

"I suppose," he remarked at last, "that you did tell me you wanted to go ice-skating."

Her eyes widened. The request hadn't been serious, in no small part because it truly had seemed impossible. "Right now?"

"Yes, right now."

Her grip tightened on his hand. "But we don't have skates."

"That does pose a problem." The laughter in his eyes suggested he was teasing her. "Over here."

He guided her to a bench, where he had her sit sideways and put her legs across his lap. Then he bent over her feet, muttering an incantation. To her amazed delight, a pair of silver skates began to materialize over her shoes, translucent and glowing, as though formed from starlight.

A realization crept over her. Nathaniel couldn't simply do whatever magic he wanted on a whim. If he didn't already have a spell memorized, he had to recite the incantation from a grimoire. According to him, he hadn't gone ice-skating since he was a child—

which meant he must have learned this spell for her, and obviously not within the past thirty minutes. It was something he had been planning for weeks.

Holding her breath, she looked up at him. Silver light spilled between his fingers, illuminating his grave expression of concentration, his entire focus narrowed to his hand hovering above her ankle. She couldn't tell if the tingling warmth where the backs of her legs rested across his thighs was real or imagined, or even some effect of the spell.

She tried not to look disappointed as he lifted her legs down and started in on his own skates.

"Try standing up," he said once he'd finished. "How do they feel?"

He took her by the hands and guided her to her feet. Her ankles wobbled. "I'm not sure," she replied, alarmed.

"You'll get the hang of it quickly. At least I hope so, because if you fall, you're taking me with you." He leaned his cane against the bench, transferring his weight to Elisabeth's arm.

She gathered her courage. Balancing on the silver blades, she tottered over to the pond, yelping as they reached the icy surface and one of her feet slid out from under her. After a moment of frantic pinwheeling, Nathaniel's grip steadied her. He looked perfectly at ease on his skates, though she knew it was an illusion; he couldn't put any weight on his bent knee, and could only walk without the cane at a stiff, painful hobble.

Slowly, they cast off with their arms linked. Giddy elation seized Elisabeth at their smooth rush forward across the ice. It seemed they were moving very fast, even though she suspected they weren't. The hedges and statues and snow-blanketed gazebo sailed past; the icy wind buffeted her ears. As they neared the pond's edge, she nearly drove them straight onto the bank until Nathaniel applied his weight and guided them into a gentle curve.

Their skates left twin trails of luminous silver streaks, which gradually melted away behind them. By the time they'd gone around the pond three times, she no longer felt unsteady on her feet. She had begun to acclimatize to the feeling of coasting across the ice, perceiving it as a controlled glide instead of a reckless slide, punctuated by the rhythmic scrape of their blades. With every movement, she could feel Nathaniel's muscles tensing and shifting against her shoulder through the swaddling layers of their coats. Eventually their patterns grew more daring—they tried turning in tighter circles and even going backward, tracing silver arcs over the pond's surface. Their laughter echoed across the garden.

She wasn't sure how long they skated, only that she never wanted it to end. Exertion had warmed her through, making her immune to the cold except for her ears and the tip of her nose. At last they scraped to a stop, revolving slowly to face each other, hand in hand.

Nathaniel was out of breath, the color high in his cheeks. The magic's dwindling glow etched his angular features in silver and turned his eyes to quartz beneath his long black lashes, wet from melted snowflakes. Elisabeth stared. Sometimes it was painful just to look at him; his beauty slipped a knife between her ribs in a thrust of hopeless yearning. It didn't strike her, until his hand came up to cradle her face, the glove's leather cool against her flushed cheek, that he might feel the same way.

"Elisabeth," he said, "it has occurred to me recently that I may have neglected to express my feelings for you out loud."

Despite the jolt of half-anxious, half-pleasant surprise that went shooting through her, she felt a lurking note of suspicion. "Did Silas have a talk with you last night?"

"That is entirely beside the point. You know that I—that I love you. Apparently I've never expressed that to you before, in what one might call a traditionally verbal fashion."

"You made that awful joke about poetry after collapsing on Lady Ingram's rug," she pointed out, unable to resist.

"I wouldn't say I collapsed. I was heroically recumbent. It's a traditional vantage from which to make a romantic confession."

Despite his tone, he seemed slightly desperate. Shyness gripped her. "Nathaniel—I already know how you feel. You do tell me that you love me."

He looked lost. "I do?"

"Not with words. But you stayed up all night just to make me breakfast. You nearly singed off your eyebrows de-cursing the armor."

"Only because of the wards," he said. "I suspect Aunt Clothilde was right about one thing. I haven't been the suitor you deserve."

"I don't want a suitor," she replied, emotion coursing through her. "I just want you, Nathaniel, not life-endangering acts of heroism, or—or priceless treasures, or even starlight in a jar. I haven't changed my mind. I still love you. I think it's possible I might love you even more than I did three months ago."

He looked away, blinking. "Perfectly understandable. I recall I had a certain odor at the time."

"Nathaniel."

He faced her again, his expression raw. Then he said, "Damn the house," and kissed her.

His mouth was shockingly hot in the cold. Elisabeth's thoughts shattered like a dropped glass. She brought her hands up to bury them in his hair, only to find herself patting ineffectually at his head with her mittens. He laughed into her mouth as she tore them off and threw them, one after the other, uncaring where they landed. When she clenched her fingers avengingly into his hair, he redoubled the force of his kiss. She slid a few inches backward on her skates, propelled by his leaning weight.

Even though she knew this was a ridiculous thing to think, she felt as though kissing were something they had discovered—a marvelous secret that only they knew, and were inventing as they went along. His gloved fingers fumbled at her coat's buttons (too overcome, she realized with a thrill, to use magic) and then his hands slipped inside, sliding up her waist, the feel of his gloves against her nightgown astonishingly provocative even before he dropped his mouth to her exposed neck, lush heat interspersed with the occasional scrape of teeth.

"I forgot to mention how devastatingly attractive you are," he said. "Don't laugh. It's true. You're brave, strong, an unstoppable force for good—which I admire even though it's very inconvenient to me personally— and you drive me mad with lust, especially when you're stomping around in that giant suit of armor."

Through a haze of sensation, understanding dawned. "I had no idea you found that sort of thing so stimulating."

He groaned, his face buried against her neck.

"I could wear it next time," she continued, mischief sparking. "You know how to put it on me."

"Elisabeth." His breath was furnace-hot against her skin. "Stop. You're going to kill me."

"It's too bad we didn't save any of Aunt Clothilde's gowns for you."

They were clinging to each other, shaking with laughter, slipping across the ice and making failed attempts to resume kissing when it happened—a feeling like a great rush of wind sweeping across the gardens, except her hair didn't stir, nor did the bushes or the branches of the trees.

Her breath caught. "What was that?"

Nathaniel's expression had sobered. He pressed a hand to his chest as if to make sure his heart was still beating. "I'm not entirely sure. I've never felt anything like it before. It felt like magic, but . . . strange. Ancient." He looked past her, and she followed his gaze. At first she saw nothing, until she realized that that was the difference: nothing. Brassbridge's lights shone steadily in the distance. The manor's swirling cloud of debris had vanished.

"The Lovers' Pact," she whispered. "Nathaniel, it was real."

He glanced down at their skates. "We've completed the third task," he murmured, as though hardly able to believe it.

She touched his face, guiding his gaze back to hers. His eyes fell to her lips. A dizzy rush of anticipation seized her, a feeling of infinite possibility, as though doors had been thrown wide within her, revealing undiscovered rooms and corridors that she hadn't known existed, waiting to be explored. Then she blinked, and frowned.

"Nathaniel," she said, pierced with sudden urgency. "What day is it?"

He opened his mouth to answer, then paused. They looked at each other in dread. Ten days had passed— and the Midwinter Ball was tomorrow.

NINE

NATHANIEL'S FIRST ORDER of business was to hurriedly spell the outer hedge to three times its usual height, walling off the manor before the reporters gathered outside, and none too soon: by the time Elisabeth had sheepishly collected her mittens, the horizon already held a watery tint of dawn.

Silas awaited them in the ballroom, clearly having spent their time outdoors preparing. He whisked Elisabeth away at once, helping her dress and arrange her hair at triple the usual speed, then pressed a dressmaker's card into her hand—"Lady Tremayne's," it read in silver foil, with an address embossed beneath—accompanied by a page of instructions for the seamstresses, written on creamy stationery in his spidery, antique hand.

"I consider this cheating," he remarked as he led her through a servants' passageway to the carriage waiting hidden outside, "but I fear we have been backed into a corner. It would be a grievous offense for you to be seen in the same gown that you wore to Lady Kicklighter's luncheon."

She didn't understand what he meant about cheating until she reached the shop, after a detour to retrieve Katrien from the Royal Library for moral support. Spilling out of the carriage, she found herself standing before a black-and-silver storefront whose sparkling windows showcased hats, gowns, and lace gloves levitating in midair. Fashionably dressed young women crowded the sidewalk, pointing excitedly and shading their eyes to peer inside.

It wasn't just a dress shop; it was a *magical* dress shop. Unable to banish the memory of Aunt Clothilde's enraged petticoats from her mind, Elisabeth felt her hand itching for Demonslayer's pommel. But the shop's interior proved decidedly nonthreatening: it was decorated as a sort of parlor, with plump velvet armchairs upholstered in primrose velvet and bouquets of hothouse flowers decorating the tables. She didn't have time to form any more observations, because as soon as the door's bell tinkled in welcome, the seamstresses descended upon her and Katrien like sparrows on a scattering of crumbs.

Once Silas's instructions were produced and read, they found themselves promptly ushered to a private salon behind a curtain. The next thirty or so minutes passed in a whirl of measurements and fittings, the operation conducted with flawless precision by Lady Tremayne herself, a handsome woman with vibrant red hair caught up in a net of pearls. It took some time for Elisabeth to get used to the enchanted measuring tapes, which whipped through the air of their own accord— the work of a sorcerer, Lady Tremayne explained, who provided charms for many of the shops on Lacebrick Lane. Katrien managed to capture one in her satchel when no one was looking, no doubt to be smuggled home for further study.

After a week trapped in Thorn Manor, the sound and color and bustle left Elisabeth dazed. She was relieved when the seamstresses finally disappeared into their workshop, chattering, to do the alterations while she waited, eating her way through a tiered dessert stand of miniature iced cakes and chocolate creams. Reconnoitering at the staff door, Katrien reported that the needles were enchanted too, diving in and out of the fabric like silver porpoises.

By the time they finished, enough boxes were brought forth to require the services of a porter, who nearly tripped over the curb carrying them to the carriage, unable to see over the teetering mountain of beribboned packages. Alarmed, Elisabeth wondered exactly what Silas had written down in his instructions.

It was still early enough for her to carry out a swift errand after dropping Katrien off at the library. Upon emerging from her destination, a grand domed and pillared building in the theater district, she was sweating beneath her coat.

An unseasonable warmth had descended over Brassbridge. On the ride home she passed children playing in the streets, couples taking strolls with their faces tipped toward the sky, linens being aired on balconies in the sun. The air held the soft, dreamy quality of early spring. No one seemed to be in a hurry to get anywhere; even the cabdrivers tipped their hats at each other instead of dashing onto the pavement in competition for a fare.

When she returned to the manor—avoiding the front, where a parade of carriages lined the street behind the crowd of reporters attempting to peer through the hedge—it was to find the windows thrown open and the floors sparkling. The streaming prisms of sunlight seemed to strip an extra layer of dust from every surface, leaving the air as clear and luminous as crystal. The mouthwatering wafts of steam emanating from the kitchen suggested Silas was at work inside, so after helping the beleaguered carriage driver heft her packages through the servants' passage, she roamed past the manor's billowing curtains in search of Nathaniel and Mercy.

She guessed that she would find them preparing the ballroom. As though the sun had passed behind a cloud, a sudden melancholy enveloped her. The room as she had first seen it, with its lowered chandeliers and dreaming air of mystery, would now exist only in her memories. She would never dance with Silas again over tiles untouched in her lifetime, her footprints in the dust traced by moonlight. Even her memory of that night might fade as the years passed. Already she felt the details slipping from her mind.

Silas will remind me, she thought. *He will tell me all of it again.* Yet somehow this only intensified her sorrow.

Her strange mood evaporated when she reached the ballroom, replaced by a bright flush of wonder. Nathaniel was nearly finished with the decorative illusions. And the theme he had chosen . . .

The walls and pillars had been turned to rough castle stones like the princess's tower, with rose vines twining up them, blooming in a dozen shades of pink and red. Arbors arched over the windows overlooking the terrace, laden with blossoms; more flowers spilled in frothy cascades from the chandeliers, home to nesting songbirds. Elisabeth nearly gasped when a hare darted across the floor in front of her, only to vanish through one of the mirrors.

Slowly approaching the glass, she found that it captured her own reflection as usual, but instead of reproducing the ballroom behind her, it showed her standing in a wild forest glade. The next contained a tower bedroom, gauzy curtains blowing, and the one after that a wildflower meadow home to a grazing unicorn, which bolted like a skittish deer as soon as her reflection entered the frame. Each scene came straight from a fairy tale.

Nathaniel hadn't caught sight of her yet. He was striding down the center of the room, formally dressed in a deep emerald tailcoat and black waistcoat embroidered with a pattern of thorns. In his free hand he held an open grimoire, his brow furrowed as he flipped through the pages. Elisabeth recognized it at once as Austermeer's Complete Fairy Tales.

In the same breath, she understood what the grimoire had been trying to tell her. Nathaniel was an orphan—hence *The Orphan Prince*. He had been the one to mark *The Three Impossible Tasks*. Despite his disavowal of fairy tales, he must have read it in his study the night after she gave him the first task.

He loves me, she thought, a tingling warmth spreading throughout her body. It was one thing to hear the words said out loud. But to have felt the ancient magic of the Lovers' Pact sweep through her—that was another thing entirely.

Still unaware of her scrutiny, he paused to brush his hand over a pillar, drawing forth more blooms from the rose vines climbing up its stones. His hair hung tousled about his face, and his intricately tied white cravat was already in considerable disarray. Imagining Silas's reaction, Elisabeth grinned.

As though summoned, the demon appeared beside her, lifting the tag on the package in her arms for a cursory glance at its label.

"I trust that Lady Tremayne's work is up to standard," he commented, "though I dare not succumb to optimism." He looked slightly harried. A few white strands had come loose from his queue, and a dish towel lay folded over his shoulder. "Master Thorn," he added, raising his whispering voice to its limits, "the guests have arrived, and are waiting on the street outside."

Nathaniel whirled around, the rose he had been coaxing into bloom evaporating in a puff of green smoke. "Already? It isn't even—"

"It is three o' clock, master."

Elisabeth frowned. "I thought the ball wasn't supposed to start until eight."

Nathaniel roamed over, already lifting his chin for Silas's assault on his cravat. "Some of the guests are visiting from outside of Brassbridge, so they expect us to host them for the night. Silas, if you've ever wanted to strangle me, now would be the time."

"How many sorcerers are there?" Elisabeth asked in alarm, recalling the line of carriages she had glimpsed stretching around the block.

"More than you would think, but most don't bother attending. The real nuisance is that anyone from a sorcerous family is invited. An entire ecosystem of useless cousins survive on these sorts of events, hoping enough of their relatives die that they inherit a demon before everyone stops feeding them appetizers."

"Which raises the matter," Silas said with thinly veiled impatience, "of how we are to manage serving the guests. Naturally I myself cannot act as a servant, though I may continue cooking out of sight. I trust none of the guests will venture past the scullery."

Elisabeth frowned. "Won't they expect to see you?"

"Not in human form, mistress. It is customary for demons to remain in their animal forms in public. I cannot glamour sorcerers into believing I am human, and few outside the Thorn household have seen me as I am now." *Seen him as he is now and survived,* Elisabeth thought, remembering the men in the alley. "For a brief period of time I have no doubt I could escape notice, as

I did under Nathaniel's illusion at the Royal Ball, but there I was only one servant among many. A sorcerer was not as likely to pick me out, should they bother noticing a servant at all. Here, I would be alone."

"You forgot me," Mercy said in a small, tight voice. She had drifted over gripping her mop, looking as though she were facing her own execution—and no wonder, Elisabeth thought with a plunging heart. An event this size would require dozens of servants to go smoothly.

"Nonsense," Silas said. Elisabeth tensed, uncertain, until he ushered Mercy into the drawing room, where she and the carriage driver had left the parcels in an enormous heap on the card table. Checking several more of the tags, he selected one and handed it to her to unwrap.

"It would be better if you enjoyed yourself, for even the most heroic efforts of one servant are unlikely to rescue us from our current straits. I took the liberty of guessing your measurements."

Mercy's eyes widened. She had folded aside the paper to reveal an expanse of shining russet satin, the lace collar embroidered with pearls. She gazed at it for a moment in hopeless longing, then lifted her chin, battening down her desire. "This is a lady's gown," she protested. "It wouldn't be right. I shouldn't . . . I can't . . ."

"Certainly you can. We shall truthfully inform the guests that you are a friend of Mistress Scrivener's, like Miss Quillworthy, who I expect will be making an appearance also, no doubt to the consternation of any sorcerer misfortunate enough to be cornered for scientific analysis."

Elisabeth saw that she still wasn't quite convinced. "I'm an orphan, Mercy. Until last year, my best dress was a hand-me-down that barely fit. If I can wear a gown like that, so can you."

Mercy hesitated. Then she turned back to the gown in wonder, running her fingers disbelievingly over the satin with a telltale redness starting around her eyes.

"Perhaps you would like to prepare," Silas suggested, passing her a few smaller packages whose size indicated accessories—silk stockings, gloves, a shawl. She nodded shortly in thanks as she made for the stairs, swiping her tears away only after she had turned around.

Elisabeth's heart swelled with gratitude toward Silas. She was more glad than ever that she had made the extra stop on her way home, though she dared not touch the slips of paper tucked inside the breast of her stays, in case he noticed and guessed where she had been.

"It is not such a kindness as you might imagine, mistress," he remarked, gazing in the direction of the foyer. "Through no fault of her own, Mercy is not trained in the style to which these guests are accustomed. It would be dreadful for me to watch."

Beside them, Nathaniel fatalistically surveyed the heap of packages, their silk ribbons and striped paper glistening in the sun. "I suppose I've paid for this, have I?"

"Indeed, master. Perhaps you should attend to your magisterial duties more diligently for a time. Now, if you will excuse me."

As he turned to go, Nathaniel caught his arm, arresting him in the act of removing the towel from his shoulder. "Silas, don't. Stay. Let them see you."

Silas's colorless eyebrows climbed. "Master, it isn't done."

"Who cares what's done? I certainly don't."

"So I have observed," he said dryly.

Nathaniel bent, bringing their faces level. Instead of lowering his eyes, Silas gazed coolly back. "Silas, you *saved the world*. Every person waiting outside this house is alive because of you."

"I did not do it for them."

"All the more reason why you shouldn't have to hide." Nathaniel's grip bunched the fabric of Silas's sleeve. "To lurk in the shadows while they eat your food and gossip about you, just to make them feel comfortable—"

"Master Thorn." Silas held up a hand between them. "I care not what they think or say. And I must ask, if you possessed the option of spending the next twenty-four hours in the form of a cat"—his eyes flicked meaningfully toward the windows, where the crowd waited outside, teeming, Elisabeth imagined, with a multitude of starving cousins—"would you not gladly consider it?" He smiled at Nathaniel's expression. "So I thought."

"Another pace back," Nathaniel said, evaluating the distance between themselves and the front door. "That should do it. Are you ready, Scrivener?"

Grimly, she eyed the windows. Movement stirred

beyond the curtains. "If anything goes wrong, I have a sword."

He took her in, his eyes sparkling. "That's my girl."

Before she could react, he spoke an incantation that made the doors slam open, accompanied by a gust of wind. Immediately, a clamor of voices drowned out the sound of the chandeliers' crystals tinkling overhead.

Elisabeth received only a brief glimpse of the line of guests waiting outside, the reporters shouting beyond, and the fleet of carriages clogging the street, some of them elaborately painted and emblazoned with coats of arms, before a voluptuous middle-aged woman in glamorous violet silks swanned inside, enveloping them in a cloud of perfume.

"Nathaniel, you've left us waiting for *hours*!" she wailed. "I'm positively *wilting*, darling!" To Elisabeth's astonished delight, she proceeded to seize Nathaniel and plant a kiss on each of his cheeks, leaving smudges of rouge behind. Then she rounded on Elisabeth and gave her the same treatment, as though they were already the best of friends.

"Auntie Louise," Nathaniel said. "How excellent to see you. I see you've met Elisabeth. Is that your porter?" He seemed in a hurry to move her along.

Auntie Louise, not to be deterred, admiringly took Elisabeth by the arms. "Darling, you're so tall! And the marvelous things I've heard about you! No wonder you stole our dear Nathaniel's heart." She lowered her voice to a conspiratorial whisper. "We thought he would never court a girl after that mortifying incident with Lady Gwendolyn . . ."

Nathaniel coughed, snapping his fingers to magick her trunk upstairs. "Friend of my mother's," he explained once she had gone, wiping the rouge from his cheeks. "Not actually my aunt by blood, though I didn't realize that until I was seven . . . ah, hello, Wilfred. The appetizers are that way."

The man in question muttered an ambiguous thank-you as he skulked past. Nathaniel was then occupied for a moment by the arrival of a troupe of musicians, whose instrument cases caused a jam in the hallway. Judging by his look of surprise, she suspected he had forgotten to book them; no doubt Silas had taken care of that minor detail.

By the time the arrivals thinned, Elisabeth's head swam with names and titles. Though none of the visiting sorcerers had brought their demons inside, she had seen a fascinating array of demonic marks, ranging from claws to pointed ears to a rare sorceress who wore a single scale like a beauty mark on her cheek. It warmed her to discover that Nathaniel did have a family, of a sort—people like Auntie Louise, who cared for him dearly, even though he had obviously kept them at arm's length since his parents' deaths. Perhaps she could help change that. She wouldn't mind hearing what Louise had to say about Lady Gwendolyn.

When the introductions finally concluded, she was grateful to escape upstairs to her quiet room, where Silas awaited her. As he helped her prepare, the sky darkened beyond the cracked-open window. The distant urban melody of wheels rattling over cobblestone, urchins hawking the evening paper, and church bells sonorously pealing the hour mingled with the muted conversations of guests passing in the hall outside.

Once Silas had finished pinning her hair into place, he took her hand and helped her upright, turning her toward the mirror.

Elisabeth's throat tightened. The lamplight's glow cast a golden sheen over the gown's dark blue silk, embroidered with a pattern of bronze plumage at the bust. A diaphanous layer of chiffon floated over the skirt, embroidered with more glimmering feathers, as though captured in midfall as they drifted to the ground. It was a gown fit for a fairy tale, but it was more than that too: blue and bronze were Great Library colors. The embroidery matched the greatkey that hung on a chain around her neck, and the feathers evoked the Collegium's crossed key and quill.

Only a few months ago, she wouldn't have been able to wear these colors. They would have reminded her of her broken oaths, or of her time imprisoned in Ashcroft's manor, forced to wear a blue gown as he interrogated her nightly in his study. But now she saw that they hadn't been ruined for her. She was proud to wear them again.

Silas was watching her closely, waiting for her reaction: he couldn't read it, she realized. Impossible though it seemed, he didn't know for certain whether the gown had been the right choice. "Thank you," she said, taking his hand. "It's perfect." And then, "Silas . . ."

Something had occurred to her while he'd pinned her hair. He had been practiced at caring for her from the very first night she had arrived in Brassbridge. Those weren't skills he could have learned from raising Nathaniel—how to lace stays, or modify a dress, or properly fix her long hair. She thought of Charlotte and the mysterious owner of the ostrich room. She remembered the drawings she had chosen not to look at in the servants' quarters, and wondered.

"Never mind," she finished softly. "Perhaps we can talk about it another time."

He didn't reply. When she glanced at him, his yellow gaze was distant, seeing something beyond their reflections in the mirror. Just as she was about to ask if he was all right, he returned to himself and stepped back, lifting her gloved hand to his lips.

"Enjoy yourself, Miss Scrivener," he said. "Should you need me, I am never far."

Leaving her room, she was startled by the light and life that filled the manor. Below, the guest-filled foyer glittered like a jewel box, its multitude of colors dappled by the spangled light of the chandelier. Voices and laughter spilled up the stairwell. Not since the time of Charlotte and Alistair, she felt certain, had the house held this much joy.

She stood for a moment with her hands on the rail, gathering her courage as though she were about to plunge into water. It was then that she spied Katrien's dark braid weaving through the crowd. Katrien spotted her at the same time and hurried up the stairs, her skirts gathered in her hands, resplendent in a dusky rose gown that hugged her figure and complemented her brown skin. Elisabeth stared; she had never seen Katrien wearing anything but her apprentice's robes.

Drawing near, Katrien said, "Tell Silas to warn me in advance the next time he delivers a mysterious package to the dormitory. Whenever I do that to someone, it's booby-trapped. I nearly threw this dress out the window."

As soon as it grew apparent that neither of them had seen Mercy, they went down the hall to knock on her door. After a lingering pause, she opened it looking like a stranger in the russet gown, her hair carefully arranged and her cheeks flaming scarlet. They helped her choose between the pair of shawls Silas had ordered for her, and then the three of them went downstairs together.

It wasn't as easy to find Nathaniel as Elisabeth thought it would be. She got stopped every few paces to have her gown complimented, her hand shaken vigorously, or to be submitted to questioning—what was her opinion of Ashcroft's sentencing? Was it true she had once slain a fiend with her bare hands? And when were she and Nathaniel planning on getting married? She very nearly suspected some of them of being undercover reporters.

She gradually became separated from Katrien and Mercy, but a few stolen glances reassured her that they were having fun. Mercy had found Beatrice, Dr. Godfrey's assistant—the two of them were deep in conversation, earnestly holding each other's hands. Meanwhile, Katrien stood within a huddle of girls having an animated discussion about Lady Tremayne's dress shop. A squeal rang out when Katrien told them about the enchanted sewing needles, attracting a sepulchral glance from Chancellor Sallow, the thin, lugubrious-looking sorcerer appointed to serve the remainder of Ashcroft's term. He had established himself in a recess of the dining room, much like a spider constructing a web, and had succeeded in gloomily cornering a pair of younger sorcerers who looked desperate to escape his clutches.

Elisabeth didn't have a clue as to Nathaniel's whereabouts until she heard someone ask through the music,

"But where the devil are your servants, Magister Thorn?" in a baffled voice slurring with drink.

The bodies shifted enough to reveal Nathaniel leaning against a rose-twined pillar near the ballroom's entrance, holding a glass of champagne, encircled by guests like a prince holding court. If she didn't know him so well, she would have thought he was enjoying himself, but she recognized his discomfort in the forced sharpness of his smile.

"That's just the thing," one of the onlookers near Elisabeth whispered. "I've heard he doesn't have any. For six whole years, he lived with no one but his demon. That poor Miss Scrivener. What must it be like for her?"

"It's very nice, actually," Elisabeth replied. "The demon makes excellent scones." She brushed past into the ballroom without pausing to take in their shocked expressions.

Ahead, Nathaniel was scanning the crowd. His eyes casually passed over Elisabeth, then snapped back to her immediately. Seeming to forget the existence of the guests—one person was still trying to talk to him, oblivious—he pushed off from the pillar, his dark gaze unwavering. She was already overwarm from earlier, and the look he was giving her didn't help; she felt flushed and sweaty, not remotely beautiful. But as he came forward to draw her into the center of the ball-room to dance, every worry fled her mind, for at that moment she was where she most wanted to be in all the world, in the arms of someone who loved her.

They danced for the better part of an hour, during which time she didn't step on Nathaniel's foot even once, before the music paused and she wandered off in search of refreshments. Bottles and glasses had been laid out on a long white cloth in the dining room, and guests were pouring their own glasses with exaggerated care, laughing at the novelty. Everyone was tipsy, the air suffused with a generous spirit, people reaching to help their neighbors whenever a glass nearly toppled or a bottle spilled. Warmth fogged the windowpanes, blurring the city's lights outside.

When she returned to the ballroom, buzzing with contentment, Nathaniel was absorbed in conversation with a young man—an extremely handsome one, with curly blond hair and dimples that flashed when he smiled. He looked nervous, fiddling with his cuffs. Intrigued,

Elisabeth ducked behind a potted plant to watch.

"I truly don't hold it against you," the young man was saying, heartfelt. "I wish you had written back, but I understand the circumstances weren't ideal. It's only, considering what happened between us . . ."

As he spoke, Nathaniel seized someone's half-empty champagne glass and downed it in one swallow, ignoring the guest's feeble cry of protest. "Felix," he said in a strained voice, trying not to cough, "while the kiss we shared in Lord Ingram's linen closet was profoundly memorable, I regret to say I now have certain commitments."

"Commitments," Felix repeated tentatively. Elisabeth didn't blame him for looking like he was wondering whether Nathaniel understood the meaning of the word, or had just chosen it at random, as though pulling it from a hat.

Nathaniel reached out to pat his arm. "It is incumbent upon me," he said gravely, "to inform you that I am no longer a bachelor."

Felix's shoulders drooped, crestfallen. She felt a twinge of sympathy. "There isn't any hope for us, then?"

Nathaniel had just opened his mouth to answer

when a vibration ran through the floor. A cluster of empty glasses discarded on a tray nearby began rattling threateningly, as though in the warning tremors preceding an earthquake. A discordant note sounded from the orchestra; a few confused murmurs went around the ballroom at the manor's ominous juddering.

"I'm afraid not," Nathaniel said, looking hunted. "The truth is that I am—engaged."

The manor subsided. All nearby conversation ceased at once.

"What?" said Felix.

"What?" said Elisabeth, standing up from behind the potted plant.

Nathaniel shot her a desperate glance. She saw him mutter a few words under his breath—an incantation—and felt something cool encircle the ring finger of her left hand, which suddenly wore a ring, obviously a Thorn family heirloom, worked in silver with a huge emerald stone. After a flash of stuttering terror, an extraordinary joy swept through her, as though she had just fallen off a precipice and discovered she could fly.

"Right. I forgot." Grinning, she lifted her hand. "We're engaged."

EPILOGUE

AS THE GUESTS danced, Silas descended into the gloom of Thorn Manor's cellar. He welcomed the smells of damp stone and mildew as an improvement over the miasma of tawdry perfume filling the air above. It seemed to him that human fashions grew more vulgar with every passing decade; now ladies purchased cheaply made gowns and gloves at the new department store on Staircross Avenue, which to his horror showed every sign of being the future. He regretted his immortality, as it ensured he would live to witness crimes even greater still.

He passed barrels and wine racks on his way to the small warped door fitted into the stone, which led down to the dungeon via a corkscrew stair. Deep beneath the manor, the wards hummed like the lifeblood of a hibernating dragon. Silas knew that placing a hand against the wall would reveal a faint vibration where they lay nearest to the stones. He abstained, having no wish to soil another pair of gloves.

The week before last, he had found it a simple enough matter to wake Clothilde Thorn's magic from its dormancy, and was pleased to find his efforts yielding the anticipated results. Without intervention, Master Thorn would have stalled for years, and Silas was impatient to plan the wedding. In fact, he had already chosen the flowers.

With a demon's sight, he had no difficulty making out his surroundings in the lightless dungeon: the squat pillars, the crude cells with their rotted doors, the soot-grimed masonry above the empty, rusted sconces. This place hadn't been used for centuries by anyone save him. A pleasant tinge of death still hung about its confines, freshest in the nearest cell, though the body that had occupied it now rested in the silt of the Gloaming River, its pockets weighted with stones.

Master Thorn and Mistress Scrivener had no knowledge of this—that the night they were attacked by fiends, he had brought Ashcroft's hired man here for questioning, and only afterward disposed of him. It had not been the quick, clean, spontaneous death that they had imagined. Silas had been thorough.

He didn't regret the subterfuge. Abstain though he might from a demon's vices, this was not the first person, or the last, that he would kill in his master and mistress's service, and it wouldn't do for their consciences to stay his hand. Especially not Mistress Scrivener's, whose righteous soul blazed from her mortal body like a corona of holy fire; a soul whose power he had tasted, and without which he would not have survived.

Halfway across the dungeon, he paused, his thoughts turning to the smell that had hung about her upon her return. Though he hadn't visited the opera in many years, he could not mistake it. She had been to the Royal Theater. He would endeavor to feign surprise when she presented the tickets to him, and it wouldn't be difficult, for indeed he was deeply touched.

His objective lay at the far end of the dungeon, graven on the stones of the largest cell, which had been equipped with iron bars in antiquity. Corroded now to nearly nothing, they protruded from the floor and ceiling like the stumps of blackened teeth. He stepped through them and surveyed the pentagram with its ancient bloodstains and grimy puddles of wax, where he had been summoned time and time again, securing hundreds of years of life from an endless succession of Thorns.

How things had changed. Then, at the height of his power, he had never noticed the chill.

Shifting the bundle in his arms, he removed his gloves and pricked his finger with a claw.

He had considered a number of ways to dispose of Clothilde Thorn's dressing gown. He had considered fire; he had considered locking it in an iron coffer and dropping it into the sea; he had considered abandoning it in the wilds to be torn apart by animals. Finally he had settled upon a fate that struck him as satisfactory.

As he bent to press the bead of blood on his finger to the pentagram's carvings, a distant cheer went up in the ballroom above. Hearing it, he smiled.

Then he spoke a name that made the very stones go silent. Had a mortal been present, the sound would have been the last they ever heard, for it would have stolen the air from their lungs and stopped the blood in their veins. Folding his hands behind his back, he watched the pentagram vanish, replaced by a pit descending into fathomless dark.

Within the abyss, scales rasped wetly over rock. A great pair of opalescent eyes shone with a corpse-light glow, illuminating piles upon piles of gleaming black coils. A hissing voice issued from the shadows like tide-water seething across splintered bone: "I am the Great Devourer, Eater of a Thousand Armies. When the world was new, I swallowed storms and drank the sea. Who dares awaken me from my slumber?"

Silas leaned over the edge.

The coils flinched in surprise. "*Silariathas?* Why did you summon me?"

"For the usual purpose. I wish to dispose of some-thing." He lifted Clothilde's dressing gown.

A long silence elapsed.

"Is that a human garment?" the Great Devourer asked.

"I fear that is the intent," Silas replied.

"I don't want to eat it."

"You are the Great Devourer. It is your purpose to consume all that lies in your path."

"Still," the serpent hedged, its eye fixing on a frill of moth-eaten lace.

The toe of Silas's boot shifted a fraction toward the pentagram's edge. Below, the Devourer cringed.

"You look terrible, Silariathas," it seethed. "You may hide your wounds from your human master, but you cannot hide them from me! The armies of the Otherworld will find you. They will tear you limb from limb. They will not sleep until they glut themselves on your flesh!"

"Strange," said Silas.

"What?" the Devourer hissed. "What's strange?"

"I should think they would prefer to live."

A moment later, empty-handed and with the Devourer's stench fading from the dungeon, Silas weighed his options. He could remain below in the darkness, with his memories for company, surrounded by the lingering echoes of death. Though he felt the cold now as he hadn't before, the prospect of biding his time here did not distress him. He considered it for a long moment.

Then he turned for the stairs, toward the light and life above.

ACKNOWLEDGMENTS

Firstly, I would like to thank my readers, whose requests for an extended epilogue inspired me to write this novella. Your continued love for this world and its characters means more to me than I can say. Because of you, the story lives on beyond its final page.

Thank you to my agent, Sara Megibow, for her wise counsel and enduring support. My editor, Karen Wojtyla, for expertly shaping this book into its final form. Thank you also to Nicole Fiorica, Emily Ritter, Bridget Madsen, Irene Metaxatos, Mitch Thorpe, and everyone at Simon & Schuster who helped usher my words along from first draft to bookstore shelves. Without their enthusiasm and hard work, this story wouldn't be in your hands.

Every day, I appreciate how lucky I am that my books have such beautiful covers. My eternal gratitude goes to artist Charlie Bowater for her illustrative work, and to Sonia Chaghatzbanian for the jacket design.

Finally, thank you to Tiffany Wang for her encouraging feedback as a beta reader; to booksellers around the world, whose critical role in connecting readers with my books cannot be overstated; and to my family and friends, whose love and support have helped me weather every storm.